MARRIED
TO THE BADGE

MARRIED TO THE BADGE

STEPHANIE JOHNSON

Urban Books
10 BRENNAN PLACE
DEER PARK, NY 11729

ISBN: 978-0-7394-8662-7

Printed in the United States of America

Acknowledgments

To my sons, who have kept me grounded, focused and on point. I love you so much. Thank you for being you and supporting me in my writing. Any and everything I do I do it for you! Tyson, you have been a blessing in our lives. We'll always love you! Tupac, you are a mess with your funny looking self.

All to often we take advantage of people who come into our lives by not accepting them as they are, respecting them for their honesty and by judging them for not being our definition of perfect. I have had the fortune of meeting someone who has added so much to my life. We accepted each other for who we are no questions asked. To know that someone is there for you, has your back, is only concerned with bringing happiness to your life and keeping a smile on your face is an unexplainable pleasure. I can't define it and don't want to. The friendship that we have is priceless and so is he! The mentality shared between us is intoxicating, often times paralyzing and I am so grateful that he is in my life. You know who you are and I love you!

To my girls Tysha and Tyshel, keep doing your thing! For those of you who don't know, they are designers who are based out in California. Go check them out at www.lockamedesigns.com.

Thank you to all of my readers, friends and family who have supported me and continue to support me.

Peace
Stephanie

Chapter One

Pier returned with all of her belongings back to her apartment last week. Two months ago she moved into her boyfriend Eric's place after knowing him for only six months. For the life of her she couldn't understand why she did such a stupid thing. She and Eric had a bumpy relationship from the door. It may have been his charm. Who knows? During the short period of time that they were together, they accomplished nothing as a couple. She allowed him to fuck up her emotions by dealing with all of his mental abuse that he'd inflicted upon her and she was in debt in the tune of over $5,000 from trying to keep up with his lifestyle.

When Eric and Pier met, they were at a club called Seductions in Asbury Park. It was the summer of 2004. Pier, her sister Corinne and girlfriends Renee and April were out celebrating Corinne's birthday. The club was packed and the music was bumping. Their heads were tight and they had bottles of champagne that they passed between the four of them so they were buzzing from that too.

They had reserved a table in the VIP section of the club. Now VIP in this club wasn't like VIP in the clubs in New York. VIP meant that they paid to sit at a table that they probably could've had without reserving. They had their own waiter who only took orders for their drinks and a small buffet right behind where they sat, that only they could eat from.

"Thank you y'all. This is so nice and I am so high," Corrine said as she sipped her champagne and danced to the music. She stood in front of their table, which was one platform up from the dance floor.

"No problem. You know how we do," Renee said.

"Corrine, here's to you," Pier said. "You are the best sister anybody could ever have."

"Aw," April teased. "Pier, do me a favor save the Harlequin shit for the chick who gives a damn. Let's go and get our dance on."

Each grabbed a bottle of champagne and went onto the dance floor. They were into their groove when a bouncer came over and busted up their party.

"No drinks on the dance floor," he growled and proceeded to take the bottles away from them.

"Oh hell no," Pier yelled. "Give us back our bottles and we'll take them back to our table." He ignored her.

"Excuse me asshole can we have our bottles back? We paid for those and we're not the only people who have drinks on the floor."

The music was blaring and Pier was yelling at the top of her lungs. The bouncer walked away from her and went over to the bar. She followed him.

"Look we heard you. You don't have to be a complete jerk and not give us our bottles back. Damn, it's my sister's birthday and we're just trying to have a little fun. I said we'd put them back on the table."

"Sorry. Those are the rules. Any drinks on the dance floor belong to me." He then turned his back to her and he sat the bottles on the bar.

Pier picked up one of the bottles of champagne and poured it over his head.

Within a few seconds, she was lifted off of her feet and carried to the door. Corinne, Renee and April were dying laughing. She could hear them laughing as they followed the bouncers who carried her ass out the door.

"Damn, can't we get our things?" Renee said as she continued to laugh.

"One, only one of you can go back and get your things." The two bouncers that carried Pier out put her down and one of them followed Corrine as she went to retrieve their belongings.

"I can not believe that you just did that. You would think we were in there slinging drugs or something. You got dudes making mad money in there and all we were doing was having a good time. Tired ass wanna be cops."

The bouncer remained quiet. He had a strong build, stood about 6'4, and had dark eyes. His eye brows were thick and he wore a low fade. He was wearing a black tee shirt that had Seductions printed on it that fit him tight and was tucked into his jeans. On his feet, were a pair of black Timberlands.

"I mean look at you. You're not all that. You probably wanted to press up on one of us and just didn't have the nerve so you and your sand box buddies wanna play us. That's cool. Punk ass."

"Pier, chill. We'll just go somewhere else. It'll be okay. Seductions isn't the only club around here," April said.

"Oh where are you going to go, the Redwood?" Lurch finally spoke.

"None of your damn business," Pier scowled.

"You know what? To be so pretty, you have a nasty mouth. Does your man allow you to talk to him like that?"

"What? Allow? My Man? What the fuck? I do what I want and my mouth is mine. Dirty or not, you shouldn't be all up in it!"

"Oh okay. I see who wears the pants."

"That's right."

"Nice, sexy, tight pants," he teased.

"Um humph," Pier shifted and rolled her eyes.

"Check her out," Renee said as she nudged April.

Pier looked over at them and wanted to laugh but kept her composure. She didn't want muscle man to know that she liked his flirtatious ways. She was buzzed, had no man, and was a tad bit horny. So she welcomed the attention, good or bad.

"Why do you have to be like that?"

"Like what? You and the super heroes dissed me and my girls."

"You can't have liquor on the dance floor. It's policy. We're liable if someone slips, falls and hurts themselves."

She looked over at him. Pier was still upset that they busted up their little party but she had to admit, he was cleaning it up nicely.

"If it were you who just so happened to fall after someone was on the dance floor with a drink, you would want to be compensated for any physical harm, correct?"

"Of course. I would get mine!"

"Exactly my point. It's our job, my job, to make sure everyone follows the rules and no one gets hurt. I'm protecting you too."

"Damn girl, he is putting it on her ass. Look at her, Renee."

"Be quiet April."

Pier did soften up a little after he explained all that mess to her.

"Can we at least get the other two bottles of champagne then? That shit ain't cheap."

"How about I take you and your friends out and you can have all the champagne you want."

"Damn. We accept," April said. "What's your name?"

"Eric."

"Ok. Eric, here is Pier's number. Give her a call and we'll have our date." April wrote Pier's number on his hand. He looked at Pier for any objection. She didn't give any.

On the way home Corrine, April, Renee and Pier laughed about what had happened. They got on Pier about how tough she was and how she changed when Eric started putting his game down. Pier liked it, she really did. She liked being carried out by the two of them and how they controlled the entire situation. Ordinarily if she flirted with a man, she could get what she wanted, but they didn't budge. And that alone turned her on.

Men who work in bars get tons of situations where they have to handle women or remove them from the bar. Pier couldn't imagine her man being in the bars, bouncing here, bouncing there and getting hit on by chicks. They're weak and when temptation strikes, almost always they give in. That's why she was single. She did what she wanted, went where she wanted and didn't have to worry about her man stepping out on her. That's something that she could not deal with. And a liar? That was her biggest issue with men. They lie and women believe every word they say. They get in the minds of women and end up controlling everything. Women give up the goods, the men put it on them and that's it, the women are hooked. They pay a few bills and women lose their minds. Women cook, clean, and cater to them only to be cheated on, lied to and played. They kiss all the right places, say all the right things, act like they are in control and committed to the relationship and then kaboom, the shit is blown up into pieces.

Corrine, April and Renee always tell Pier that she is harsh on men; that she doesn't give them a chance to prove themselves. Maybe Pier was because she hasn't met the one who was caring, passionate and honest. She wanted to, but nowadays the person you meet isn't the person that you get to know. As time goes on, they slowly change from the sales representative to the scumbag that they truly are. Dressed up on the outside and fucked up on the inside.

Pier was looking forward to this date with Eric. She wanted to see how slick his game was when they were one on one. Who knows? Maybe they would hit it off. His smooth talk coupled with his nice body might just do the trick. But one thing she knew for sure, he wasn't going to get her that easy.

Chapter Two

The date with Eric was crazy. First he took them out to eat at Carmines on Main Street in Asbury. Then they went over to the VFW. All of them had a couple of drinks there then April, Corinne and Renee went home. The VFW closed at 11:00, so Pier trucked Eric over to the Legion for an hour and had a few more drinks. She tried to keep the conversation light but Eric had other plans.

"So are you married?" He asked

"No. See, no ring," she said, as she dangled her bare ring finger in his face.

"That doesn't always mean anything, so I thought I'd ask."

"Yeah well for me it does. First I'd be sporting that five carat ring that whoever he would be bought me and second, I wouldn't he here with you."

"Sure about that?"

"You're arrogant, you think?"

"No you think," he laughed.

"Yes. I do. So are you married?"

"Seperated." He looked down.

"Well is that a good or bad thing?"

"It's definitely for the best. We just can't seem to get on the same page. She doesn't seem to be able to understand my needs. Now whether she wants to or not, is anybody's guess. I do know that I've brought it to her attention many times."

"And . . . ?"

"And she just doesn't get it."

"What is it that you need?"

"I need a woman who will allow me to be the man, someone who won't fight me on everything."

"You need a submissive."

"No."

I nodded my head yes.

"No I need a partner."

He said that so sincere. She looked into his eyes.

"How long have you guys been separated?"

"A year."

"Have you dated anyone in between?"

"I've dated here and there but nothing serious came out of it."

"And you think you're ready for a relationship, a serious committed relationship?" Pier asked as she stared him in the eyes.

"Yes. I believe that things happen for a reason and that people have a purpose in the lives of others."

"Really!"

"Yes, really." He winked.

She and Eric had a few more dates and with each date, Eric charmed her more and more. On the third date, he charmed Pier right out of her panties. From the moment she left her panties on his bedroom floor, she made herself comfortable at his place. She'd spend the night and leave in the morning to go to work. Then she would find herself right back over his house in the evenings. After about two weeks of that, bringing clothes to change into at night and for work, Pier just took over a few outfits, couple of bras and panties, her toothbrush, hair shit, all of that and felt right at home. She lived between his place and hers for about five months. Then she would stay at his place for an entire week and not go home at all. Pier and Eric had decided that they would give the relationship thing a serious chance and she moved in his place completely. She did however keep her apartment because she wanted that security of having her own place just in case things didn't work out between them.

Eric continued to work as a bouncer four nights out of the week and was a security guard at the county jail during the day. Sometimes he would come home between, sometimes he didn't. Pier would lay across the couch and wait up until he got home. Then they would make love and on occasion have crazy out of control sex that would leave them both sweating like wild animals and sprawled out on the bed.

Then all of a sudden, weird things started happening. The phone would ring once in the middle of the night and during the day someone would leave messages of heavy breathing on the machine. One day when Pier was outside bringing the groceries into the house, some chick came up to her and handed her a laundry bag of washed clothes. The woman turned and walked away and over to the next house. When Pier asked Eric about it, he told her that this girl had always done his laundry to make a few extra dollars.

"Well, I'm here now and you have the room for a washer and dryer. Why not just buy them?"

"That's a good idea," he responded.

So Pier went out and bought a washer and dryer for his place and paid to have it installed. She made it so that the girl-next-door services were no longer needed. The following week, the girl came back over and said that Eric had borrowed some money from her and wanted to know if Pier knew when he was going to pay her back.

"Ah, no doll. I don't know anything about any money being borrowed or paid back."

"You don't?"

"No." Pier got agitated.

"Do you know about his daughter?"

"Daughter?"

"Um hum. She's six months old."

"Yeah right. I don't have time for this honey."

"Okay, I can come back another day." She stood and waited for a response from Pier.

Pier stared at her and said nothing as she slammed the door in her face. She looked out the blinds and watched her walk down the stairs and out of sight.

Daughter?

Pier couldn't wait for Eric to get home. She tried not to get all worked up because she knew how women could be, especially if they wanted your man. Pier wanted to ask him what she was talking about and give him the opportunity to respond. If she went at him ignorantly, he wouldn't open up to her and tell the truth.

"She came here and said that you had a daughter and that she was with you."

"She's delusional. Okay, before you came into the picture, we did fool around but it was nothing serious. She would come over, I'd hit it and she'd be on her way. That's it. She does have a daughter, but it's not mine. The little girl could be anybody's because she sleeps around with everybody. We had a DNA test and everything."

"And what were the results?"

"Man, I told you that it's not my baby. Why do you keep on questioning me?"

"Because I want to know."

"And I told you. Now let's just drop it."

His demeanor was laxed and when he spoke, he had Pier's hands in his and looked her directly in the eyes. She was convinced that this neighbor girl just had the hots for her man and that she was jealous of her position with Eric.

"Okay baby, because you know you don't have to lie to me. We're being honest with each other right?" She really needed to know this.

"Yeah baby. Come here." He took her by the waist and sat her on his lap. Then she remembered that the girl also asked about getting some money from him that she had lent him.

"But wait, she also asked for the money that she lent you."

"Baby, I'm telling you, she's crazy. Money, I have a job, two jobs. Why would I need to borrow money from her?"

He was dressed in his uniform. Pier got turned on when he was in uniform and the way he reassured her made her even more excited. She undressed him and they made love until it was time for him to go to the bouncer gig, then they took a shower together. He got dressed and left.

Pier was in a deep sleep when the phone rang.

"Hello."

"Did Eric give you my money?"

"Look, I'm not sure what you think but Eric didn't borrow any money from you. Now I know that you guys were dealing before I came into the picture. I would appreciate it if you would stop calling and coming over here with your shit. He also told me that your baby isn't his, so quit it already."

"You know, you're right. We did mess around and I probably shouldn't be involving you in this. But I see you guys together all happy and then here I am with his daughter who he spends no time with and it bothers me. It's not your problem though. Bye." She hung up the phone.

She thought to herself that this woman was crazy. The sound of her voice was creepy. She didn't yell not once. She was as calm as can be.

Pier lay next to Eric as he slept. The conversation with that girl was on her mind heavy. She didn't get a good night's sleep because she wanted to talk about it. She knew he got in late, but couldn't hold it in any longer.

"What is her name?" Pier asked as she poked Eric.

"Who?" He got out of the bed and went into the bathroom to pee.

"The girl next door."

"Why does it matter?" He finished up and got back into bed.

"It matters because she called here with her mess again last night. I mean why would she be calling if there was no reason or if there was no truth to what she's saying."

"I told you babe, she's just jealous that you're here. We did it a few times and obviously she caught feelings and she's trying to push you away. Come here."

She sat up beside him. Part of her wanted to believe everything that he said but women just don't trip like that. If they're emotionally attached, it's not because they have nothing to do. It's because the person who they are attached to has given them valid reason to be. Some women can't handle just having sex. To them that spells commitment.

"I just need to know. The truth Eric is what I want to hear."

"What, you don't believe me now?"

"Eric, she wouldn't be calling here for no good reason. You said you had a DNA test. Obviously somebody thought a test needed to be done. She couldn't do it without your consent."

"Look, I told you already. I can't *make* you believe me. I'm tired and I'm going back to sleep."

Pier sighed and got up. She had to be to work shortly and didn't have the time to get into a full fledged discussion. But she knew in her gut that he wasn't telling her the truth.

"We need to really talk about this more. And I want to talk to you and her together."

"Whatever babe."

Pier pulled out her white linen suit, jumped in the shower, got herself together and was out the door. When she got to her car, there was an envelope on the windshield. She took it off, unlocked the car door and went to open it. When she grabbed the handle to lift it up, her fingers slipped into something. She pulled her hand out from the door handle and there was shit on her fingers and there was a diaper on the ground next to the car.

"What the fuck! Eric." She yelled as she marched right back into the house.

"Eric, get up. That bitch put baby shit on the handle of my car and I got it all over my fingers. I'm going over there right now. Get your ass up."

"What are you talking about?" He jumped out of bed.

"This is what I'm talking about." She said as she wiped her shitty hand on his tee shirt.

"Ay yo, what the hell are you doing?"

Pier walked out and into the kitchen and placed the envelope on the counter. She pulled the bleach out from under the sink along with some dish detergent. She squeezed some onto her hands then poured some bleach on them too. Pier began to wash her hands as she went off on Eric.

"I'm telling you right now Eric, I'm about to go and kick this bitch's ass."

Once her hands were cleaned, Pier grabbed the envelope, walked out, and was on her way over to the girl's house. She opened the envelope and took out a piece of paper as she walked up to her door. Pier stopped dead in her tracks.

On the piece of paper were the results of a DNA test that proved that Eric was the father of one Alyssa Jones, daughter of Regan Jones, residing at 348 Hollow Trail. It also included a child support order. This had to have been the money she was looking for from him. Pier looked up at the door and saw the numbers on the crazy girl's house. She let her arms fall to her sides and just shook her head. She felt so stupid. Pier couldn't even be mad at her because she had told Pier the deal and Pier chose to believe Eric's lies instead.

As Pier packed her bags, Eric pleaded but she wasn't listening. She had asked him twice about this girl and that baby, but he continued to deny it. He did nothing but lie to her and she wasn't trying to hear it. She felt like she had wasted enough of her time with this man and if he was lying so early in their relationship, the future would be nothing but a big lie too.

"Okay, okay. I'm sorry I didn't tell you about the baby. I'm sorry Pier."

"Eric, forget you. You're nothing but a liar and you know what, I'm better than that. I deserve better than that. I'm not wasting any more time on your ass. And what kind of man would deny his own child? Sorry ass nigga!" She wanted to cry but for what? It was a lesson learned. She couldn't believe she had dealt with months of lies but she took full responsibility because the chick had warned her from the door.

So there she was back in her apartment, alone. Pier flicked through the channels and stumbled upon her favorite show, *Law & Order*. She tossed the remote on the couch, grabbed the blanket that was on the chair and flopped down on the cushions. She was angry that Eric had gotten away with his lies for so long, even though the evidence was right there in her face. The love making they shared was a lie. His so-called commitment to her was a lie. That was it for her. She didn't want to be bothered with men anymore. If she didn't expect anything, she couldn't be disappointed, so alone was what she would be. Pier was hurt and disappointed in herself for being so stupid. She reached for the lamp, turned it off and tried to go to sleep. She closed her eyes and wondered if she would ever meet a man that was open and honest. Deep in her heart she wanted that, she really did. She wanted a man who would love her and not lie to her. Someone who provided security and wanted to be with her and her only. Pier wanted a man who was in control of his life and knew what he wanted. She wanted love.

Chapter Three

Pier took a few months to be by herself, re-evaluate her life, her job, and to try and get her priorities straight. She was alone by choice and to her surprise never once felt lonely. Eric had really made her see that pretty packages don't always hold pretty things. For a minute she beat herself up because she really should've known better. Look where she met him. He was bouncing at a bar. She was sure he ran into all types of women and had all types of one night stands. So what hers lasted six months instead of one night. She was hardly any different than those other girls.

Her days consisted of going to work, hanging with the girls and going home to an empty apartment. On the weekends, she cleaned, rearranged her cabinets and prayed that one day she would find her knight and shining armor. Sometimes Pier, Corrine, April and Renee would go out and have dinner or to the movies, anything to make the time go by.

Renee, April and Corrine were pretty good at keeping her busy when she wasn't doing her other stuff. Pier and

Corrine had always been close. The two year gap in their ages didn't affect their relationship at all. Pier was the older of the two and always kept Corrine as close to her as possible. Renee and April were their childhood friends and although they all went their separate ways to attend college, they all ended up back in their home town of Neptune.

"What are we going to do this weekend?" Corrine asked Pier while they did some grocery shopping.

"Personally, I could sit and watch a couple of movies."

"Pier, you've done that for the last two weekends!"

"Well what else is there to do?"

"Let's go out and have a few drinks."

Pier looked over at her. "I'm not doing the VFW again. You can straight forget that."

"Okay. Let's go to this bar down in Asbury. It used to be Harry's Road House. I don't remember the name off hand but I know how to get there. The dress is casual so we don't have to go all crazy trying to find an outfit to wear. Jeans will do."

"Alright, I can do that. Make sure you call April and Renee."

Renee agreed to be the designated driver. Not that any of them had planned to get completely wasted but since she's the light weight and only drank two glasses of wine max, she was it. The place was now called Red Fusions. The line to get it wasn't long, however once they got into the club, it was standing room only. There were so many men in there Renee, Corrine and April couldn't hide their glory. Pier wanted to have a drink and chill. She was done picking up men in bars.

"Grab the back of my shirt and I'll lead us to the bar."

Corinne grabbed Pier, April grabbed Corrine and Renee

grabbed April. As they bobbed and weaved through the crowd, their toes got stepped on and someone even spilled a drink on April.

"Sorry," the blond-haired blue-eyed girl yelled as she continued to dance on a pole that was near by. April just nodded and kept moving. She wasn't the violent type. None of them were, but Pier would've had a bit more attitude if she had to walk around with a drink stain on her outfit for the rest of the night.

"Who's drinking what?" Renee asked as she pulled out her money.

"The usual for me," Pier said as she turned to look at the crowd of people dancing.

"Wine," April said.

"Jack and Ginger Ale for me," Corinne sang. "I am ready to cut up!"

"Oh Lord," Pier laughed.

They found a booth over in the corner and sat down with their drinks. The crowd was mixed and the DJ was playing all 80s music.

"I've never been to this place before and why are those girls dancing with each other?"

"April, most of them do dance with each other. You never see a sister dancing with another sister."

"True."

"I'm not down with that mess," Pier said. "I know that sometimes you get into the music and start dancing with anybody, but dancing with women has never been my style."

"So you wouldn't dance with me?"

"Nope."

"Forget you then," April said. They all busted out laughing. The girls began getting on each other about their different hang-ups when a man approached them.

* * *

"Would you dance with me?"

All of them were quiet because they didn't know who he was talking to. "You," he pointed to Pier.

"Aw shoot, get him Pier," April shouted.

"No thanks. I don't like this song," she said politely turning him down.

"Ouch!"

Corinne gave Pier the wide-eyed look. Pier rolled her eyes and again told him no thanks.

"Okay, maybe next time." He walked away

"Why in the hell did you kick me?"

"Because ever since Eric you act like all men are ass-holes."

"Most of them are, but right now you're about the biggest one for kicking me, knowing full well that I bruise easily."

"Sorry. You really just need to get over that mess and move on."

"I think that she should take as much time as she needs to heal from being done wrong. I don't see any-thing wrong with laying low and regrouping. So what it's been weeks. If she doesn't mind a dry cooch, why should you?"

"You're a mess April," Pier said as she laughed. But in-side, she felt like she wanted to dance with him but didn't even trust him to do that. They'd be dancing and the next thing you know, he'd talk his talk, touch her some kind of way and she'd fall for his play. She was done being played. Eric's mess had really put her in a funk about dating again. Despite the fact that she really wanted someone in her life, she couldn't trust anyone. Her heart wouldn't let her.

They ordered a few appetizers, finished their drinks and were home by 1:00 am. The next morning, it was so beautiful outside that Pier decided to go walking. She tried to reach out to the girls but they were all still asleep.

It was 7:30 and the neighborhood was quiet. It must've rained some time during the night because all of the cars had rail bubbles on them. She loved the smell of the rain especially on a cool summer morning. As she walked, Pier could hear the birds chirp. The leaves on the trees moved gently as the wind blew. She was relaxed.

Pier sped up her pace and began to move her arms as she walked. She went for ten blocks with no interruption of step or shortness of breath. It felt good to get her heart pumping faster than usual. As she turned the corner, she saw what looked like fruit in the middle of the sidewalk. When she got closer she saw oranges, apples and a bag of potatoes at the end of the driveway of a house. A man dressed in a police uniform was moving as fast as he could to catch the falling bags that he pulled out of his trunk.

"Can I help you with that," Pier asked as she laughed.

"No," he said as he dropped yet another bag. This time onions and a bag of flour dropped. "Damn it."

"Okay, I'm going to help you anyway since I see you're having a hard time." Pier proceeded to get all of the groceries that were on the sidewalk and took them up to his porch. Then she grabbed the flour bag that burst upon impact and his onions and stuffed them back into the bag.

"Here you go," she said holding them out to him.

"Thanks. I appreciate it. You can just sit them in the trunk and I will come back for them."

"Okay. By the way, my name is Pier. Pier Rhodes."

"Kyle. Kyle Evans." He tried to shake her hand, but dropped another bag in the process.

"This just isn't my day."

"Do you always shop this early in the morning?" She asked him as she helped him pick up more of his things.

"Well I just got off. I figured I better do it now because once I lay down I'll be sleep until I have to go to work again tonight. Midnight shifts are the worse."

"Oh okay. Let me help you get these on the porch."

"Better yet can you grab my keys out of my pocket and just open the front door. That would be a great help."

Now, that was a weird request but she offered to help him and did as he asked. Pier walked up the stairs to his front door then turned to look at Kyle. It was hysterical that he was still trying to carry too many bags at once. She unlocked the door and opened it. From what she could see his house was beautiful. There was a hint of orange in the air. It smelled really good. Pier opened the screen door and put on the stoppers so that it remained opened for him to carry his things through.

"I'll leave the keys on this table by the door," she shouted as she lay them down.

"Okay, thank you."

"You sure you don't need any more help?"

"No, really thank you. You're too kind already."

"Okay, well it was nice meeting you Kyle." Pier held her hand out but then realized that both of his were full of grocery bags.

"Now how am I going to shake your hand?" He joked. "Tell you what, reach into my shirt pocket and grab one of my business cards. Please, call me so that I can take you out to dinner for your kindness."

"No really, you don't have to do that."

"It's the least I can do."

She was a bit hesitant but decided what the hell. She would have his number, he wouldn't have hers and if she decided to call, cool. And since he didn't have her phone number, she didn't have to worry about being harassed in any way. Pier saw no harm in that. She reached into his pocket, took one of his cards and bid him farewell again.

"Be sure to call me, Pier. I'd really like to show my appreciation." He stood at the bottom of the porch stairs and watched her as she walked away. She turned around.

"We'll see. Bye Kyle."

Pier tossed the card in the first garbage can she saw.

On her way back home she purposely took a different route. Pier didn't realize that she flirted with him until after all was said and done. She didn't want to run into Kyle again because she didn't want him to pick up on the fact that she had no intentions on calling him. No matter how nice he was, it would show on her face that he wasn't going to get past first base. To Pier, a man in a uniform was bad news and since she was still stuck on how Eric had lied to her, Kyle didn't stand a chance.

"That's ridiculous," April said.

"You're not lying. All you did was help the man with his groceries and he wanted to thank you by taking you out to dinner. What's the big damn deal?" Renee asked siding with April.

"I would go myself," Corinne said. "It's only dinner and you are greedy."

"Be quiet. It's just that, well, all I was trying to do was help him, not pick him up. If that were me trying to catch my apples and oranges, I would want someone to help me but I wouldn't ask them out. I would simply say thank you. And he did that so why do I need to go out to dinner with him?"

"How long are you going to hold onto what Eric did to you? He is so yesterday's news. Get over it already. All men aren't bad. Just because Eric wore a uniform and was a complete jackass doesn't mean that every man who wears a uniform is one. I mean this could be the one. If you keep turning down men because of your past, you may miss your blessing of a good man. You're too young to give up on your love life."

"April, I'm just not ready. I don't like being by myself but I'm getting used to it. I don't want to be hurt. I don't want to give my heart to someone only for them to break it. And this guy may be a good one but I don't know." Pier shrugged her shoulders.

"And you won't if you don't at least get to know him. No one said you had to marry the man."

"I guess you're right."

"Well if you don't want to see what he's about, can I get his number? I'll call him and he can take me out."

"I can't do that. I told you I threw out his card."

"Well you know what city he works for right?" Renee asked.

"Yeah."

"So call him girl, damn. Lighten up."

They were right. But after that mess with Eric, Pier didn't think she could trust anyone with her feelings. And although it would only be dinner, she couldn't seem to let her guard down. The uniform thing was an issue too. He looked nothing like Eric but reminded her of him for that reason alone. Maybe they could do lunch. It would be day time and wouldn't seem like a real date. Maybe they'll just have lunch and that will be it; never see or speak to each other again.

"That was nice of me to help him. I mean I could've

just kept walking and completely ignored that his groceries were scattered in the middle of the street." Pier paused.

"Alright, I'll go see if I can set up a lunch date tomorrow."

"Alright now," Corrine said.

"We got your back. If it will make you feel any better, we can come and sit a few tables away from you. Make sure you pick the spot."

"No thank you. I know how you guys can get. We're going to Chili's. That's all you need to know."

"This is going to be funny," Renee giggled.

"Yeah, I'm sure it is," Pier mumbled.

Corrine, Renee and April talked amongst themselves as Pier drifted into deep thought. She knew that she would have to let go of Eric and the madness he was about sooner or later. She hadn't been out on a date since him and could really use the company of the opposite sex. The girls were cool and all but Pier really wanted to spend time with a man who was interested in spending time with her and was interested in talking with her. Somebody who was articulate, smart and enjoyed the company of a good woman. If she continued to allow her past relationship to hover over her head, she may miss out on something good. Not all men were dogs so they said, and if things went well with her and Kyle, maybe her days of being alone would soon end.

Chapter Four

"Can I speak to Kyle Evans, please?"
The dispatcher transferred her call.
"Captain Kyle Evans."
Captain?
"Kyle, its Pier."
"Well, well, well. I thought I would never hear from you. I actually waited on my porch for you to walk back my way because I realized that I didn't get *your* number. How are you? I'm so glad you called!"
"I'm good. Yeah, I took the long way back home."
"Okay. So where can I take you to eat? I really do appreciate your help the other morning."
"How does Chili's sound?"
"Great. What time do you want me to pick you up?"
"I can meet you there around one o'clock."
"I can pick you up. It's the least I can do."
"No. I'd rather drive my own car."
Pier didn't want Kyle to know where she lived. She didn't feel comfortable with him coming to her house and if she drove her car, she could bail out if things weren't

going to her liking or she was bored. He didn't say anything for a moment. Maybe he wasn't feeling her driving on her own but oh well. It was her way or the highway. She didn't know this dude.

"Is there something wrong?"

He cleared his throat. "No. One o'clock is good. See you there."

When Pier arrived at the restaurant, the workplace lunch crowd was busy eating and having drinks. She walked up to the hostess station.

"Hi, table for two. I'm supposed to meet someone."

"Are they here yet?" The hostess asked as she looked at her table chart.

"I don't know." Pier looked around the restaurant for Kyle but didn't see him. She was a bit early. She looked at her watch and it was ten minutes to one.

The girl told her that she couldn't be seated at a table until her party was complete but could sit at the bar and wait. So that's what she did. She requested a glass of water and waited for Kyle to come. As she sat there, she watched the people mingle. They were laughing and talking so loud she was beginning to get a headache. A couple sat at a table and from the looks if it, they would've been better off in a hotel room. Pier sipped her water and watched them exchange kisses. It must be nice to have someone you cared for and not be afraid to show it. The couple looked as though they were in love. He held her close and she touched his face as they smiled and whispered to each other. The more she watched them, the more she wanted what they appeared to have. A loving relationship. She too wanted to be passionately kissed. She wanted to feel her lover's hands roam her body and wanted that tingle in her gut that told her it was good for her. Pier wanted to be consumed by his manliness and made to believe that she was his queen.

She moved her gaze and looked across the bar. There was Kyle. She didn't know if she should smile or break out that joint. It gave her the chills that he sat on the other side and stared at her. She wondered how long he'd been sitting there. Pier wasn't feeling that at all. He motioned for her to come over to him. She grabbed her water and purse and slowly walked over to the other side of the bar. She prayed that she hadn't opened herself to yet another whack job. He stood up and extended his hand.

"Now I can shake your hand."

"Hi Kyle," she said and sat down. "So how long have you been sitting here?"

"I've been here for about a half an hour."

"Really?" For some reason, that bothered her. A half an hour was a long time to be waiting when they weren't supposed to meet there until one. "Let's go and get our table."

"I already took care of that." He got up. "Follow me." Pier grabbed her things again and followed him towards the back of the restaurant where a table was reserved especially for them. There was a single yellow rose and a card on one of the place settings. Kyle pulled out her chair and Pier sat down. Pier went to open the card but he stopped her.

"Wait. I have one more thing." He nodded to the waitress. She left and returned with a bottle of wine and two wine glasses. She filled both glasses and left. Kyle picked them up and handed her one.

"I have a little toast."

Again, this was weird, but Pier lifted her glass anyway.

"To new friends. May we bare the fruit of great happiness. Get it, fruit?" He said with a chuckle. "Well here, here."

"You are corny," she laughed.

"But you're smiling, and it's a beautiful smile too."

"Thank you Kyle. You really didn't have to go all out."

"It's nothing really."

"So why were you here so early?" Pier picked up the menu and browsed it as she waited for his response.

"I had a business meeting."

"Oh. Why aren't you dressed in uniform then, Captain."

"Funny. I don't always have to be in uniform. Besides, none of that matters. All that matters is that you are here with me and we're going to have lunch. And there's no need for you to look at the menu, I took the liberty of ordering for you."

"You have no idea what I like Kyle."

He was controlling this whole situation. Most women would probably be flattered but she wasn't. He was going too far to make a good impression too soon. In fact, he was doing quite the opposite. He was getting on her damn nerves. But she wasn't rude and remained poised.

"Trust me, I got this." He said sipping his wine.

She sat back and watched Kyle. His movements were confident. His body language was controlled. He had no facial hair and had a bald head. He maybe stood about six feet and had no body fat. He wasn't the most handsome guy but she could tell that he got his way with women. Nothing about him spelled failure at anything.

Moments later the waitress returned with their food. Kyle ordered a variety of appetizers, a salad and one serving of pasta. They ate, talked, ate, drank and talked some more. Pier learned that Kyle was divorced and he had one daughter that he had custody of. They were married for eleven years. According to Kyle, his ex-wife became too complacent in that she would just come home and not clean the house, stopped fixing dinner and ordered out almost every night. She began to party a lot and she even stopped going to the parent teacher's conferences for Stacey knowing that Kyle couldn't make it because of his rotating shifts. After many arguments and verbal confrontations, Kyle decided that he didn't want to be married to her any longer. She wasn't providing a good home for his daughter so he divorced her and got custody of Stacey.

When Pier asked how he managed that, he said that father's have rights too. He went on to say that men can be primary caregivers and that the courts needed to know that they can be good parents and provide sometimes better than a mother could. Pier didn't have children so she couldn't fully understand where he was coming from but he seemed to keep a nice house from what she'd seen and had his stuff together. However, there were always two sides to every story.

"What is your ex-wife's name?"

"Karen. Why?"

"I was just asking. How does she feel about you dating?"

"Frankly, I don't care. Coupled with all of our other issues, she was having an affair with a local thug right under my nose. Her opinion doesn't mean anything to me."

"Wow, that's terrible. I'm sorry."

"Would you believe she had the nerve to sleep with a drug dealer, the very same scum I work very hard to keep off the streets and away from my daughter? She snuck around like a sixteen year old in love for the first time. I gave her everything. She had nothing before we met. I'm telling you, some of you are never satisfied."

"Why did she cheat? I mean most women won't step out unless things weren't being take care of at home."

"Please, Pier, I held mine down. I took care of home. All she wanted to do was go out every weekend and party like she didn't have to get up in the morning or better yet, like I didn't have to go to work every night."

"You still seem pretty upset about all of this. How long have you guys actually been divorced?"

"A year."

All kinds of thoughts ran through Pier's head. She completely understood how he felt. Eric did her wrong too by lying about his baby. He was still dealing with the mother because she would trip at the sight of her. Kyle displayed emotions that told Pier he was still connected to his ex-wife too. When he talked about their situation he tensed up. His ego was hurt that she had cheated with someone less than he was. He felt betrayed and didn't seem like he was over the hurt that she had caused him.

"Okay. How does she react if she sees you with another woman? I mean, let's just say we go out on more dates. If she sees us should I expect some baby momma drama from her?"

"I don't know. I mean she's never really seen me with another woman. With my work schedule, I date when I can. And sometimes it's late at night or early like now. I got her in check. You have nothing to worry about."

"Is that right? Let me ask you a question. Since you've been divorced, have you slept with her? And what do you mean you have her in check?"

"No we don't sleep together and what I mean by having her in check is that when we split up, there was no question that we were a done deal. There would be no reason for her to call me out on anything that I do."

"Do you see yourself married down the line and do you want more children?"

Kyle froze. Pier assumed she hit a soft spot.

"Possibly and no I'm not interested in having more children!"

"You never know, you may change your mind about having more children if you find the right woman."

"I doubt it. I don't have time for another child and Stacey is all I need."

"I don't think you're completely over it. And you know what, I feel you on that. I too was in a relationship where I experienced deceit and it's a difficult thing to get over especially when you are really feeling that person."

"Enough of that. It's depressing. Are you enjoying your food?" He reached over for the veggie patch pizza.

"Yes."

Pier was skeptical about Kyle but he seemed to be a really nice guy and at that moment, she considered going out on another date with him sometime soon.

Lunch was filling. After they left the restaurant Kyle and Pier drove over to the mall that was close by. They walked it a few times to walk off some of the food they ate. He took her hand and held it. At first, she wanted to pull it away but he held it tighter. It felt good. Then he grabbed her and pulled her closer to him. He kissed Pier on the cheek and put his arm over her shoulder. Then out of no where, he started singing to her. He couldn't sing worth a damn, but the mere fact that he tried tickled her. People stared and when he was done, a few even applauded. She could tell that Kyle loved being the center of attention. Pier was never big on that, however, it felt nice to have all eyes on them. She laughed as he finished on a high note. As they continued to walk, she put some space in between them and walked a little bit behind him. He hadn't even noticed because he was too busy profiling and taking in all the smiles that came his way. Pier just shook her head.

"You're a mess," she said as he walked her to her car.

"Why?"

"You like it when people give you a bunch of attention, don't you?

"Who doesn't? So, can I get your phone number so that we can talk and maybe get together again?"

Pier gave him her phone number, thanked him for lunch, said good bye, got in her car and left. She went home and checked her messages. There was one from Corinne and one from Kyle.

"Damn, already," she sighed. Pier called Corinne back but there was no answer so she called Kyle. She wondered what he had to say since she had just left him. She wasn't used to that and even though he was probably just being nice, Pier wasn't sure she liked it. She felt like he was being controlling again. But then she told herself that she was reading too much into it. Maybe he wanted to make sure that she got home safely.

"Hey I just wanted to thank you again for helping me and for a lovely lunch."

"You're welcome and thank you!"

"What are you about to do?" He asked.

Pier didn't really have any plans so she told him that she'd probably watch a movie or something. He asked her if he could come and watch it with her but she told him that she was a little tired and wanted some alone time. It was hard to just have someone over after being alone for so long and besides, just because lunch went good didn't mean that she wanted him to know where she lived just yet.

"Call me when you're finished."

"Okay." The phone beeped. "Hold on Kyle." She clicked over and it was Corrine. Pier clicked back over to Kyle and told him that she would call him later.

"Thanks again Pier and I am so looking forward to

getting to know you better. You seem like a really sweet person, someone that I would love to have in my life."

"Wow, thank you Kyle."

"Bye Pier."

"Chat with you later Kyle." She smiled as she returned to Corrine's call. Kyle sure was a gentleman and knew how to make her feel good. Pier liked that he wanted to see her again and that he said he wanted to get to know her. Maybe he was different. Maybe just because he liked to make sure things were in order doesn't mean he was a control freak. Maybe, just maybe she found her man . . . her other half. She was looking forward to seeing him again too.

Chapter Five

"So how was lunch?"

"Hello to you too. You just couldn't wait could you?"

"Come on, spit it out," Corinne whined.

"Lunch was interesting. I learned that Kyle was married. He has a daughter and her name is Stacey."

"Really? That's nice I guess. Are you ready to deal with a man that has a child?"

"Why wouldn't I be? He's not my man. We went on a lunch date."

"Are you going to go out with him again?"

"You know, I don't know. I gave it some thought but he had the whole lunch date planned, from the table that we sat at to the food that I ate. Don't you think that's a bit controlling?"

"Why are you reading into it like that? Why can't it be that he really appreciated you helping him and wanted to show you how much? Pier you need to lighten up. It's nothing wrong with a man showing you that kind of attention. Enjoy it girl."

"Sike, I'll go out again with him." Pier started to laugh.

Again, Corrine was right. Pier had never had a man treat her like that and after Eric she could use a little pampering.

Pier hung up the phone with Corinne and called Kyle back.

"Hey Kyle, are you asleep?"

"No. I was just sitting at the computer."

"I called to tell you that I had a really nice time at lunch."

"So did I. Does that mean that we can do it again or perhaps do dinner?"

"Yes, we can do dinner."

"Or better yet, I'm having a little get together this weekend. Why don't you come and meet my friends."

"What kind of get together?"

"Just a little party."

"Okay, sure."

Kyle and Pier talked for a little bit longer about different things. He went into more detail about the other problems that he and his wife had. She was a trip. In addition to what he'd told her earlier, he also said that she would leave his daughter with the neighbor so that she could go out on the nights that he worked. One time she left her there all night and didn't come home until the morning. Since his divorce, Kyle said that he pretty much stayed to himself and dated occasionally. He wanted a committed relationship but had yet to find a woman who could deal with his hours at work. The women that he did hook up with came in late and left shortly after. No one stayed the night, especially if his daughter was home and no one got the keys to his place.

* * *

The morning of Kyle's get together, the girls went and had their hands and feet done. Pier mentioned the party at Kyle's house.

"I want to go," Renee commented.

"You can. I don't think that he'd mind. I'm sure that there will be a few single officers there."

"Okay, well count us all in."

When they pulled up to Kyle's house there were cars lined up and down the street. They got out, walked up to the door and knocked. A heavy set white woman answered the door.

"Hello,"

"Hi, I'm Pier and I'm here for the party."

"Okay, you can follow me." She led them to the back where Kyle and his friends were. There was music and lots of food and the tables had beautiful flower center pieces on them. She yelled out to him and he came over. He gave Pier a hug and took her hand. He held it in the mall but he was amongst his friends now. She didn't want anyone to think that we were together like that, so she tried to slide her hand out from his as she gave a little smile to Corrine, Renee and April but he held on tight. If she tried any harder, she thought she'd be drawing attention to herself and she didn't want that.

"Pier, I'm so glad you could make it. And who are these young ladies?"

"This is my sister Corrine and my girlfriends April and Renee."

"Well, okay." The look on Kyle's face was a mix between being "I invited you not them" and "whatever".

"Come with me, I want to introduce you to a few people."

"Will you guys be okay?" she asked them as Kyle was

pulling her away. All three of them looked at Pier and didn't respond.

"Did you see the look on his face?" Corrine asked Renee.

"That was rude," April commented.

"Yeah, well, we're here to support her so let's just go get something to eat and be nice, okay girls?" Renee persuaded them.

They walked over to a table that had all kinds of food, cheeses, fountain drinks and a host of other things that made it onto their plates, then found a table and sat down.

"Everybody's potato salad isn't that good. I wouldn't be eating that if I were you."

"Oh please, you're being a little neurotic Corrine," Renee said.

"I'm just saying."

As they picked at their food they looked around the crowd of people and noticed that most of the men who were in uniform were consuming alcohol. Their clothing was disheveled and they were acting rowdy. They were drinking beers, mixed drinks and taking shots at a tiki bar that was set up. There were women walking around half dressed, big and small, and were giving lap dances to the men. Even a woman police officer got a lap dance.

"Okay, what in the hell kind of party is this?" April asked with a funny look on her face.

"This is some freaky mess. Did Pier know that this guy got down like this?"

"I have no idea. But look," Renee pointed, "look how he has Pier all hemmed up next to him. The dude he's talking to is staring at her like she's chopped meat."

"I'm ready to go."

"Me too," April and Corrine agreed.

* * *

The three of them got up, barely touching the plates they made, and walked over to Pier.

"Hey girl, can we talk to you for a minute?" Corinne more demanded than asked.

"Yes you can," she said. Pier tried to release herself from Kyle's hold but he wouldn't let her go.

"Kyle, give me a minute, I need to talk to my girls," she yanked her arm from him.

"What's wrong ladies? You're not having a good time?"

"Actually we just need to talk with Pier for a moment, if that's okay with you."

"Kyle, I'll be right back." Pier, Corrine, April and Renee walked to the front of the house.

"Yuk, Pier, what kind of party is dude having here? Did you know it was going to be all like this?"

"No I did not. Trust me, I'm not feeling this either but how can I politely tell him that I want to leave?"

"Politely? Damn that. Let's just go. You don't owe him anything. You see all of what's going on back there?"

"Maybe they just got off and are trying to unwind. Eitherway I am rather uncomfortable."

"And do you see those women back there winding down and carrying on?"

"Yes girl. Let me think," Pier said and battled with herself with whether or not they were making more of the situation than it was.

"Look, if you want to stay, you can. All I'm saying is that we want to go. We aren't comfortable and don't want to stay, so can we get the keys?"

"Okay, I'll tell him that we're leaving."

Pier walked over to Kyle and pulled him to the side. She told him that they weren't comfortable being there and that they were going to leave.

"Are you serious Pier? They're just having a little fun. They always act like that when they get together. They mean no harm."

"Dead serious Kyle. I understand that. It's just not our type of party."

"Fine. I understand. Why don't you and I go inside and spend some time by ourselves. Will that make you feel a little bit more comfortable? I really don't want you to go. If your friends want to leave okay, but you're my guest and I want you to feel at home."

"I don't want you to leave your friends just to hang out with me. That's not right. Have your party and we can get together another day."

"I won't hear of it. Let me excuse myself from them. Your friends, if they still want to leave, that will be even better because then I can have you all to myself. How does that sound?"

"Are you sure? I don't mean to be a pain."

"Of course I'm sure. Handle them and I'll handle my friends."

Pier did want to spend time with Kyle and when he offered to leave the party to go inside and spend some one on one time with her, that made her feel special. She spoke to the girls.

"Okay. You can take my car. I will call you when I'm ready."

"You're staying?" Corrine asked, clearly agitated.

"Yes. We're actually going to leave the party and go inside to hang out. I'll be fine. Don't worry." Pier tried to convince them but they didn't buy it. Something about this whole thing bothered the three of them and they wanted no part of it.

Pier reached into her purse and gave them her keys. She wanted to stay and have as good a time as she could with Kyle. It was thoughtful of him to want to spend quality time with her.

"I'll call you guys when I'm ready."

"Yeah, yeah," Corinne waved her hand as she, April and Renee got in the car. Pier began to walk back into the party when Kyle came from out back. He walked up to Pier and gave her a hug. He squeezed her so tight that she couldn't breathe.

"Wow, what was that for?" She asked.

"That was for staying and trusting in me."

"Well I better be able to trust you or you will have hell to pay," she said as she gently punched his arm. Pier was serious as hell though.

"Baby, you just don't know my friends. Sometimes with a job like ours, we need to let our hair down so to speak. It's hard being out there on the streets. We aren't allowed to be ourselves, joke around or have fun like the rest of folks. Let's go back to the party." He took Pier by the hand and led her to the backyard and to the bar.

"We'll take two white wines please."

"I don't drink white wine Kyle."

"You'll like this one. It's from my boy, he made it himself." Kyle pointed over to one of his officer buddies who was being caressed by one of the naked women.

"Kyle, what's the real occasion for this party? This is really tripping me out."

"Why do you ask?"

"Because it's weird back here. I mean you have all these people, mostly men, being seduced by these women and I don't know it just seems funky to me."

"Funky? Actually, it's my divorce party."

"Divorce party? I thought you said that you've been divorced for a year already and you're just now having a party? And what makes you think that I would want to come to your divorce party?" She immediately regretted not leaving with her friends.

"I just haven't had the time. You know how it is with my schedule and everything. Is what's happening here offending you?"

"What exactly is happening here Kyle?" She shouted. "And yes I'm very offended!"

"Nothing. It's just a bunch of grown folks having a good time and celebrating my single status with me. That's it."

She sipped her wine and looked around. There were half the amount of women there as men and they were all sitting at a few tables on the other side of the yard.

"Why don't you go and entertain your company and I'll go and sit with the other women who aren't flaunting their goods all over the place."

"Okay do that. I will see you in a bit. And thanks for understanding."

Pier walked over and took the last seat available at a table near the back of the house. All of the talking stopped and all eyes were on her. They stared at Pier but she wasn't intimidated. She said hello, received no hello back, and then sipped her wine as if they weren't there. Then one spoke.

"So who are you here with?"

"I'm sorry?"

"Who did you come to the party with?"

"My girlfriends but they left because they weren't feeling all of that," she said pointing at the female officer at the far end of the yard feeling on one of the male guests.

The woman laughed and said something under her breath.

"Excuse me, did you say something?" Pier stood her ground.

"I said they're smart." The woman got up and walked away.

"Don't pay any attention to her. She's a little angry because Kyle dumped her a while ago. I was surprised she even came. He had a lot of nerve even inviting her but that's always been Kyle's style. He wants what he wants and no matter how bad he dogged you out, you keep on giving it to him."

"If he broke up with her, what could he possibly want from her and why did he invite her?"

"Control. I'm Linda by the way, Kyle's attorney."

"Attorney? And you're good with being at a party like this?"

"What's wrong with it? It's all grown folks."

"I just met Kyle and I had no idea that he was like this at all."

"Like what? He's being a good host. Do you see him doing anything wrong? These are all his friends. The entertainment is for them. Loosen up honey and enjoy."

Pier looked off into the crowd of people. The music was low and you could hear the different conversations going on. At first glance you wouldn't notice the groping that was going on and the verbal masturbation that was being exchanged between most of them. She had never been around such free spirited people and was feeling more and more uncomfortable the longer she stayed. Pier sat and took in every move, sound, word and whatever else was going on.

"What's your name?" Linda asked. She was an attractive African American woman. She wore little makeup, had short hair and was a little on the heavy side. Actually, all of the women there were a little on the heavy side she had noticed.

"Pier."

"That's a nice name. It's different. Can I get you an-other glass of wine?"

"Sure. That would be nice but you know what, I don't like this one. It's the one that his friend made."

"There's more in the house. Follow me." Pier followed Linda into the house. They went in through the back door and right into the kitchen. It was all white with stainless steel accents. There was a woman in there, the same one who answered the door, cleaning up the kitchen. Linda introduced them.

"Monica, this is Pier."

"Nice to meet you," Pier greeted her.

"Hi there," Monica said as she gave a fake smile.

"Monica was my assistant. We've done lots of work for Kyle and we've become very good friends, but she left me to become a nanny to Kyle's daughter."

Monica was the only white woman there. She stood about 5 feet 9 inches or so and was huge. Everything about her was enormous. She cleaned that kitchen like she was the woman of the house. Her hair was short with strands of gray throughout. She walked with a slight drag of her left foot and had beady jet black eyes.

"She's closer to Kyle than I am, you know being younger and all. They like to leave an old sister out," Linda joked with Pier as she stood against the counter. She pulled out a bottle of wine from the refrigerator and opened it. Monica took it upon herself to get three wine glasses and sat them on the counter.

"Oh, you're joining us?" Linda asked.

"No, you know I don't drink wine. This is for Kyle, I see his glass is empty."

A flag went up in Pier's head. It's okay to have friends but Monica was acting like she was more than a friend to Kyle. She pulled out another bottle of wine from the mini wine refrigerator that sat in the corner and popped it open.

"Umm I have to ask this. You can see that Kyle's glass is empty from here?" Pier really wanted to know.

"Actually, I just know his drinking routine."

"How so? I mean have you fixed his drinks all day? Are you his," Pier paused, "his server for the day?"

"No, I don't think so. Kyle and I are friends, really good friends. Hopefully that won't be a problem for you."

Linda watched as Monica and Pier exchanged words. Pier refused to back down. This overstuffed ravioli-looking white chick was trying to punk Pier and she was so ready for her.

"The problem won't be with you being his friend. I think it will be when he and I are chilling and you're bringing us both glasses of wine. How does that sound?" Pier had a wicked smile on her face.

"Well I won't!" Monica yelled.

"Monica," Linda jumped in, "relax. Pier is Kyle's company and you need to respect that."

"Yeah respect that," Pier added.

"You can be that, his company for the day or whatever. But we're friends, friends like you will never know so guess what, you can pour your own wine while I take my friend another glass."

"Monica, I can't help but feel a little bit of jealousy from you. I mean, are you worried that my being with Kyle will change or interfere with your friendship with him? You can't be that insecure. But then again," Pier got closer to her, "when you have a little extra weight that you just can't seem to drop no matter how much exercising or cleaning you do, you can get emotional at the slightest things. I can take Kyle his wine."

Pier took the bottle of wine and the extra wine glass

and walked out. As pissed as she was, she couldn't let either Monica or Linda know it. Pier wasn't stupid. It was more than obvious that there had been some type of emotional attachment, whether then or in the past, between Monica and Kyle. She didn't appreciate being put in a position where she had to defend herself over a man that wasn't hers. She heard Monica and Linda talking as she left the room, but Pier refused to show her ass just yet. She could see, however, that she would need to do so if Monica didn't pipe it down with her mouth or if Kyle didn't put her in check. But Pier was ready because whether she was his woman or not, she would not be disrespected. Pier wasn't worried because she would get to the bottom of things with Kyle at a later time.

Chapter Six

"Monica, relax. They never last. You know that you and Kyle will always have that special friendship," Linda said rubbing Monica's shoulders as she cried hysterically.

"I don't know why he feels the need to flaunt his women in front of me. First he invites his ex-girlfriend. Then he has a date on top of it. I know we'll never be together like that again, but I can't help how I feel about him. He knows this and just ignores it."

"You have to get your feelings under control honey. You can't just give him what he wants any time he wants it. That's the problem. You're always there for him no matter what and obviously that's not working for you. Look at him," Linda took Monica over to the window where she could see everyone mingling and getting closer including Pier and Kyle. "Do you really think that he's concerned with you sitting in here upset and carrying on while he's out there having the time of his life? Girl, I don't know what to tell you. Both of you are my friends, but at some point you have to look at this situation and wonder if it's going to kill you if you stay in it."

"I can't just leave him alone Linda. I'm the only real friend he has. All of those people out there don't know him like I do and when all of the food and alcohol is gone, they will be gone too. Not me. I'm going to be here for him." She wiped her face with the dish rag. "I'm not going anywhere."

"Suit yourself Monica, but I really think you need to give it up. He's not going to see you the way you want him to see you, ever. He didn't divorce his wife to be with you like he said. He needed you to vouch for his character and you did. He needed you to act like you were a live-in nanny so that he could get custody and you did. He manipulates you all the time and you continue to allow him."

"No he doesn't. I'm his friend and I care about him. He cares about me too otherwise he wouldn't let me stay here like he does. He wouldn't ask me to house-sit when he goes on vacation so I don't care what anyone says, he does care about me."

"Okay Monica," Linda threw up her hands. "Whatever you say and now that you mentioned it, you're still staying the night over here? Why?"

"Because he wants me to. Why do you think he gave me one of the guest rooms?"

"Are you still having sex with him, Monica?"

Monica bit her bottom lip and smiled. "He sneaks into my room when I'm here every now and then."

"That's why you're acting like a strung out fool. What the hell is wrong with you? You're just setting yourself up for a let down. Girl listen, like I said I'm cool with the both of you but I can't get with this dysfunctional relationship that the two of you have going on. It's like he uses you for sex when he doesn't have anything else going on and you just allow him."

"We have a bond, a special bond that no one will ever understand."

"Get out Monica before someone gets hurt for real," Linda warned her.

Pier couldn't get to Kyle fast enough. She politely pulled him from a conversation that he was having with a few of his friends.

"Not only do you invite me to a party that is off the chain with sex, you invite an ex of yours and have another angry ex, from the way she's acting, in your kitchen. What kind of mess do you have going on here?"

"Another ex? Who are you talking about?"

"Monica."

He laughed but Pier didn't find anything funny.

"What is or was the deal between you and her?"

He went on to tell Pier that they met at a work-related function. At the time, Monica was a dispatcher at the same police station he worked at. Romances at the work place were shunned upon even though more than half of the police department was sleeping around. Whether it was with fellow officers, dispatchers or administration, affairs were being had. Some even had sex with the women that they arrested.

One night, when there wasn't too much action going on, Kyle came into the dispatch room. Monica was the only dispatcher working. With the exception of another captain who was asleep behind closed doors, Kyle was the only one inside at the time. He was the Watch Commander for that evening. She had asked him out for drinks and that was when it started. Monica didn't ever see him as someone that she would be interested in but his smooth talking changed her mind. Whenever possible, they slept together. He would leave work and go to her place before he went home.

Monica was single, had no man, hadn't had sex in God only knew how long and was horny as all hell. She thought that she and Kyle could get theirs off and keep it moving. Little did she know that she would get hooked to the ding ding and wouldn't be able to let go. From the first night they had sex she'd been his side kick. Any chick that he dealt with outside of his wife at the time had no idea that he was doing Monica too. She liked it that way because if anyone found out, she could be fired from her job. When it got to the point where he wanted to have sex with her more, he moved her into his house. He insisted that they weren't having sex any longer and that she was there to take care of the house and his daughter.

"Kyle, I truly hope that you aren't lying because I would hate to find out that you were still sleeping with her."

"Baby, trust me, we are so over."

Monica poured herself another glass of wine and watched as everyone was having a good time. Tears rolled down her face. Linda was right. Kyle could care less how she felt about him. Monica knew that they would be the perfect couple. Aside from being a bit overweight, she was smart and could keep house. His daughter Stacey liked her and was comfortable with her around. But that didn't matter to Kyle. No matter how cool they were, how good Monica was to his daughter, Kyle would never be seen in public with a woman like her. She drank the wine until she finished it all. She made her way up to her room and stretched out across the bed. Monica cried at the thoughts of Kyle and Pier being together.

* * *

The guests were thinning out and only a few were left. The music was turned off and Kyle and Pier began cleaning up the backyard. By then, she was feeling pretty good.

"This was a weird kind of party."

"No it wasn't. You're just not used to how I do things. Look at it this way, if you ever throw me a party, you know the kind of party I like. That's how I am and will be and any woman of mine will stand by my side and make sure I'm happy. That is, if she really loves me."

"Why are you like that?"

"Like what?"

She shrugged her shoulders. "Controlling."

"It's hardly controlling. It's being secure in my position and knowing what I want. If you don't like what I like, there is no need to waste my time. So you can call it controlling if you want, but I hardly see it like that."

"I guess, but it can be a little bit much. Like I said I had a nice time overall. Thanks for inviting me."

He looked up. "Most definitely. I mean I'm sorry that you didn't get a chance to hang out and talk with my friends. They really are cool peoples."

"I came here to hang out with you," Pier said softly touching his nose. He came closer to her and kissed her lips. They began to caress each other.

"Maybe we shouldn't do this out here," Pier stopped.

"Cool. Let's get this mess cleaned up. I'll get these last few guests out of here and then we can go inside and relax."

Pier finished throwing all of the left over food, paper goods and other mess away. They were completely done in a half an hour. Once the last guest left, Kyle walked with Pier inside.

"Looks like someone was having a party in here while

we were partying out there," he commented on the empty bottles of wine that were left on the counter.

"I know, right? Monica takes your friendship pretty serious, huh?"

"She can be a little over protective sometimes, yes. Part of that is my fault. For a long time she was the only female friend that I allowed around me. While I was going through my divorce, she was there for me and during that time she caught feelings."

"Well did you guys talk about them? I mean was she, is she, under the impression that you feel other than what you're telling her? She just seemed a little bent that I was here and made me feel like I was invading her space."

"Don't worry about her. She'll be fine. Come over here and give me a kiss."

Pier leaned over and kissed Kyle passionately. He grabbed her by the ass and squeezed her closer to him. Pier could feel his manhood hardening and immediately got aroused.

"Spend the night with me," he whispered.

"Oh I don't know about that. What about your daughter?"

"Don't worry about her. She'll be asleep. Let's spend some time." He licked her lips then cupped her breasts and gently pushed them together.

"Umm that feels good, Pier."

She closed her eyes and allowed herself to be taken away by Kyle's seductive touches. He felt so good.

"I need to take a shower Kyle, but I didn't bring any change of clothes. And I need to call my sister and tell her that I won't need a ride home tonight."

"No problem. I have some extra sweats you can borrow and use the phone in the bedroom. I'll go run the shower for you. Okay baby? With your sexy self."

She smiled as he led her to the bedroom. He started the shower for her and gave her the cordless phone so that she could call Corrine.

"Get undressed and get in the shower. I'll meet you here in a few minutes."

"Okay Kyle." Pier was so turned on by his smoothness.

Kyle walked out of the room and closed the door all the way. He leaned his ear up against Monica's bedroom door then softly knocked. When he didn't get an answer, he went in.

Monica was knocked out from all of the wine that she had and was unaware of his presence. He closed and locked the door behind him. As he pulled down his pants and started to masturbate he softly called her name.

"Monica, are you awake? Monica. Monica."

She shifted positions and was now on her back. Kyle walked closer to her and spread her legs.

"Monica, let me get some of that big ass girl. You know how we do. Give me some of this." As he talked to her, Kyle took off her pants and panties. He spread her legs and spoke to her again.

"Damn girl, you must've known that Daddy was going to come and break you off some of this dick. Look how wet you are." He touched her and played with her clit. Moments later she opened her eyes.

"Kyle no. Not anymore."

"Come on now, what are you talking about? You know how we do. Give me some baby."

Between being drunk and wanting Kyle to take her, Monica didn't put up any more of a fight. She spread her legs as she haphazardly took off her top and bra. Large breasts fell to her sides and Kyle went to work on them. As he sucked her nipples, she wrapped her short stout legs around his body forcing his erect penis inside of her.

"Yeah, it's real hot in here. How's my pussy doing? Did you enjoy yourself today?" With each stroke came another question, but they went unanswered as Monica took all of what he was giving.

While Pier was in the shower, she thought about Kyle's explanation of his and Monica's relationship. No she wasn't his type of woman, but it was something about her that turned him on at some point. It was fishy to Pier how Monica reacted when she realized that Pier was there for Kyle. Her reaction wasn't that of an ex who had moved on.

Pier washed her body and then her hair. She wasn't too worried about how it looked because her natural curls made good for any occasion. The shower was running cold and she wondered where Kyle was. Just as she was about turn the water off and get out, he came into the bathroom.

"Oh no you don't. Let me wash you."

"But I already washed up. I was ready to get out."

"So what. I want to feel your body soapy. I bet if feels sexy."

"The water is about to turn cold, Kyle."

"I'll warm you up." He got undressed and jumped into the shower. They caressed each other and lathered each other up. Pier let her head fall back as he kissed her neck. He slowly pushed her back onto the walls and spread her legs.

"Can I love you?"

"Love me?" She laughed

"Yes, can I make love to you?"

Pier looked at him. She had to admit, he was turning

her on and she wanted him just as much as he wanted her.

"Yes."

With that, he entered her slowly. He winded to the left until her legs were off of the floor. Then he took them and held them up by his forearms.

"Damn baby I could get used to this pussy. Yeah it's real hot in here."

"Yes, Kyle."

"Yes, right. Can you get used to me taking you like this every night? Huh?" He stroked her harder. "Turn around." He ordered and turned off the water.

He spread Pier's cheeks and entered her warmth again. She propped herself up as high as she could so that she could take all of him.

"That's right, give me this."

"Make me cum Kyle."

"Oh trust me you will." He adjusted her so that her feet were off the floor again and her ass was as high as she could stand it without slipping off of the edge of the tub. He pounded into her pussy and made her come like she never came before.

"Damn Kyle, you're really loving me. You feel so good. I'm gonna cum."

"Yeah."

"Keep on, don't stop.

"Yeah!"

"Kyle I'm cuming on you. Right now."

"Yeeeeaaaaaaaaaahhhhhhhhhh!!!" He sped up his stroke until he felt her pulsation.

"Oh, oh my God. Oh Kyle."

His short pumps told her that he came too.

"Damn girl. I guess I was backed up. I came hard."

He put Pier down and helped her get her balance. He

softly kissed her on the lips and turned the water back on.

"It's going to be cold."

"Last one to wash up makes the popcorn."

The following morning Pier woke up to an empty bed. She looked up and saw clothes set out for her on the chair. She got up put on the tee shirt and pair of boxers and went into the bathroom.

"Damn, he's prepared for everything." On the bathroom sink was a toothbrush and facial cloths. "This shit is so weird, but I like it." She brushed her teeth and washed her face. Then she wet her hair, styled it with her fingers and made her way out of the bedroom.

Pier followed the voices, one of which she knew was Monica's and when she came into the kitchen, Linda and Kyle sat and drank coffee as Monica made breakfast.

"Ah look at my sleeping beauty." Kyle went over and gave her a kiss. Pier was surprised to see Linda there. In fact she got a funny feeling in her stomach that made her cringe. She didn't understand why Kyle had Monica there all the time and now she woke up to Linda too. She felt that he was being insensitive to her being there.

"Morning," Monica said in a more pleasant voice than the day before. "Can I get you some coffee?"

"No thank you." Pier wanted to say something so bad.

"Are you sure? I made it myself," Kyle sounded disappointed. Since he said he made it, she accepted the offer. Monica began to make it but Kyle took the coffee mug from her and made it for her himself.

"How did you sleep?" Linda asked. "And don't worry I'm not staying long. I came for some leftovers."

"Well, thank you. I was tired. I guess those two glasses of wine really did me in."

"Yeah I know what you mean. I drank almost an entire bottle and whew, I had the best sex dreams of my life last night," Monica added. Pier really wasn't interested in anything she had to say.

"Is that why you're in such a good mood this morning?" Linda asked.

"I guess it is. Gotta get it any way I can you know."

"I guess," Linda said.

"So what's on the agenda today baby girl?"

"I don't' know. Normally I would've gotten my walk in by now but it's way too late for that. I need to call my sister and see what time she can pick me up."

"Don't worry about that. I can take you home."

"Monica what time will breakfast be done?" Kyle asked.

Monica tightened her jaw. Kyle waited for an answer. Not ten seconds passed and he asked her again. Linda shook her head.

"I don't know. If she's in a rush maybe you can take her to the diner on the corner."

"My baby isn't eating at any diner. Right baby?"

"It's no big deal Kyle. I'm not that hungry."

"I won't hear of it. Monica makes a mean omelet and you will eat before you leave."

"Monica, let's hurry it up a little. Come on Pier. We'll be in the den."

The den was right next to the kitchen and Pier could hear Monica and Linda talking. She had a feeling that they were talking about her but she didn't say anything as she didn't want to make a scene. She remained cool.

Linda tore into Monica.

"That's just what I'm talking about. You just let him treat you like shit!"

"I can't help but laugh Linda. Little Miss Pier thinks she has the captain wrapped around her bony little fingers. But let me tell you this, my big fat white legs was wrapped around his lean body as my lips and clit were wrapped around his big black rod, okay. So she can act however she wants." Monica moved closer to Linda and whispered. "He was fucking me last night."

"What? Where was she?" Linda tried to whisper.

"Who knows? I was gone girl but had slept most of the wine off. I don't know what time he came into my room. All I do know is that he was talking some kind of mess and talked himself right between my legs."

"And you let him?"

"Hell yeah I let him. The both of them can act like they're shit don't stink but I know the deal. He can treat me however he wants people to see him treat me, but who does he come running to first when he needs some good stuff? ME! That's right, this big white pus . . ."

"Please don't. And you seem mighty proud."

"Whatever Linda, like I told you, he may not want me like that but he wants me like that."

"Yuk! I'm out of here. Later Kyle," she yelled as she left.

Kyle jumped up and went into the kitchen. Pier stayed on the couch and finished watching television.

"Where did Linda go?" He asked Monica.

"I don't know. She didn't say." He grabbed a piece of bacon and came up behind her.

"You liked it didn't you? Huh? You liked how I came in your room and fucked you while you were passed out."

"I wasn't that passed out."

"Oh yeah? So what did I do to you?" He asked. "You already know. You better stop before your little girlfriend comes in her and sees you."

"She's alright. She's relaxing watching a movie. So tell me. You liked this dick?"

"Yes."

"Umph, I know you did. You feel it now. Feel how hard it is."

Monica put what she had in her hand down and reached behind her. Kyle still had his robe on but had nothing on under it. Monica reached and pulled out his dick.

"Rub it."

She moaned as she did what he said.

"Want to taste it?"

"Yes."

"Turn around and kneel down."

Again, she did as she was told. She knelt in front of him and took him in her mouth. He gently pumped her mouth full of himself and was hard as a rock.

"Girl, this is what I'm talking about. Suck it. Make me shoot all over your mouth." Monica quietly slurped until he let off a load onto her face.

"Okay. Okay. You like that right."

"Yes," she licked her lips.

"Now finish making my breakfast baby. I'm sure Pier is hungry by now."

Pier got up and went into the kitchen. Just as she walked in, Kyle was walking out. He was fixing his robe. He grabbed Pier and wrapped his arms around her. He danced her into the kitchen and told her that breakfast would be ready in a little bit. Pier danced along.

"Where is Monica?"

"She's over there."

Pier didn't see her. Monica knew better than to stand up and start running her mouth, so she opened the cabinet and shuffled a few pots to make it appear that she was getting ready to finish cooking. A satisfied Kyle continued to openly flirt with Pier, completely unconcerned with how Monica was feeling. Monica on the other hand knew where Kyle was going with Pier. He liked her and was going to make her a part of his life.

Chapter Seven

Monica sat on the kitchen floor. She was fuming with jealousy as she reached up on the counter for a dish towel and wiped her face of his cream. She knew it was wrong how he treated her but she loved him, loved him like no one ever could. Kyle knew this and took every opportunity to tease her, play with her mind and have sex with her. Monica knew that Kyle had no interest in being with her on any serious level but that wasn't how she felt about him.

She collected herself and finished breakfast. Against her will, she walked into the den where Pier and Kyle lay on the couch and announced that the food was ready.

"Thank you Monica. That will be all."

Monica walked away.

"She's the nanny for your daughter?" Pier still wasn't convinced.

"Yes, come on." Kyle took her by the hand.

"So she's here when she gets off from school?"

"Yes, and she's here in the morning too. Please," He pulled out a chair so Pier could sit.

"Really, how is that?" This was getting more and more interesting to Pier as the conversation went on.

"What can I say, she's a great nanny to Stacey."

"That's interesting." Pier grabbed her napkin and placed it on her lap.

"Why is that so interesting Ms. Pier?"

"I don't know. Yesterday when Linda introduced me to her, she didn't seem too pleased to meet me. Like I said, it almost seemed as if you and her had something at one time that was more serious than what you are telling me. She gave me big attitude."

"That's Monica for you. She stays here during the week so it's almost as if she thinks my house is hers. Hand me the butter please. The more comfortable she is the more comfortable my daughter is. Don't worry about her. She'll just have to get used to you being here."

"Used to me being here? What makes you think that I'll come back?" Pier teased as she picked up her fork.

"You didn't have a nice time last night?"

"I had a wonderful time. I'm a little dry right now but I had a nice time. I especially liked the shower. Are you that sensual and seductive all the time?"

"Of course. Especially when I'm with someone that I'm really feeling. That would be you." He pointed and softly touched her nose.

Pier smiled. They ate their breakfast in silence. When they were finished, Pier helped Kyle clean up the kitchen.

"I think I'd better be going. I'm sure my sister and two nosey friends are wondering where the heck I am. And you really don't have to take me home. I can call one of them to pick me up."

"No, I insist."

"Okay. If you insist. Do you have a bag for me to put my clothes in from yesterday?"

"No. In fact you can leave them here and they can get cleaned during the week."

There was no point in trying to disagree with Kyle. He would only talk Pier into his way. She left it alone and went to the back to grab her purse. As she walked past one of the rooms, she heard a bumping sound. She slowly pushed the door open. Pier poked her head in but didn't see anything. She continued to Kyle's room. On the bed was a bag with her clothes in it, and next to it was her purse and keys. She got her things and went back into the front.

"Well I'm ready to go Kyle."

"Let me get some clothes on and I'll be ready in five minutes." He went into the back.

"I'll call my sister in the meantime and let her know that I have a ride home."

When Kyle got into his room, he closed the door behind him only to find Monica there, naked and waiting for him. She locked the door

"We're not finished," she said as she pushed him until he fell back onto the bed. Then she jumped all of her 275 pounds onto him and rode him. He was soft at first but as she started winding her hips, he grabbed her ass and kept her on top of him as much as possible. Her ample breasts hung and he latched onto one with his tongue. That excited Monica but what excited her even more was the fact that Kyle's little Pier was in the other room and had no idea that she was fucking him.

Fifteen minutes passed and Pier was still waiting for

Kyle. She was growing more and more impatient by the minute.

For someone to be so much in control, he sure has no idea what five minutes means, she thought as she looked at the pictures in his living room. There were lots of pictures of a little girl, which she assumed was his daughter and lots of commendations on the wall from his job, as well as pictures of Kyle in uniform.

When she couldn't wait anymore Pier went to Kyle's bedroom. Just as she was about to open the door, the door opened and there stood Monica with Kyle's bed sheets in her hand.

"Where is Kyle?" Pier was impatient.

"He's in the bathroom getting dressed. I was about to leave but then forgot to change the linen on the beds. I'll be out of your way in a minute."

Pier went into the bathroom and let into Kyle. She wasn't comfortable with Monica being around and she popped up at the most inopportune times. Her presence gave Pier the creeps and she just wanted to leave.

"Kyle, don't worry about it, I'm going to call my sister and catch a ride. Talk with you later."

Pier walked out of the bedroom and used the phone in the kitchen. She called her sister and got no answer. She had no desire to stay there any longer especially with Monica there, so she walked out of the house and began walking home. Monica came running behind her.

"You forgot something," she said as she held up her bag of clothes.

Pier turned around and walked back up to the door. She took her clothes from Monica.

"Is your ride coming?"

"Yes. Thank you." Pier turned to walk away.

"Mine came too!"

"Look I don't know what your," Pier turned back around to speak but her words were shut down as Monica slammed the door right in her face.

Kyle came from the bedroom. "What was that noise?"

Chapter Eight

"Well you're a better person than I am. I would've given her a big piece of my mind," Corrine argued.

"It's weird, I'm telling you. This woman hated the fact that I was there."

"It's not unusual that a woman has a crush on her best friend. I mean she does live in his house, smells him, probably washes his underwear, smells those too. Cleans his bedroom, looks in his sock drawers, smells those. She does take care of his daughter so they are close in some sense."

"I can handle that, but you guys had gone already. You should've seen how she acted when his other friend, actually his lawyer, Linda, introduced us. She'd like to scratch my eyes out. Linda though, she seems cool," Pier said

"Does he have a lot of female friends?"

"I didn't gather that from the party, but that doesn't mean anything. I don't know if I could deal with that, but then again friends are friends. Almost always you can tell whether or not someone has had dealings on a sexual level with somebody or not and Monica is making it known that they have had some kind of intimacy between them."

"Maybe she's just being over protective. I mean she does take care of the man's child. And she can't help but to take care of him too. If she cooks for his daughter, I'm sure she cooks for him too. What, she makes him get his own food? No, she's taking care of that household and you obviously pose a threat to her. I wouldn't take it too seriously until you know where you and Kyle are going with your relationship. Speaking of which Missy, who do you think you are spending the night out with him? You hardly know him."

"I know Corrine, but he made it so inviting. And guess what? We did it."

"You hoe!" Corrine joked.

"And it was good. We did it in the shower. He was real excited girl. He had me all bent up so that the water ran down my back."

"I am not mad at you girl. Did you use protection?"

"No."

"Umm, I don't know about that one. I would be a little more careful if I were you."

"I'm sure you're right. The last thing I want is to become pregnant. I'm going to chill for a while. Back to work tomorrow."

"Alright. Talk with you later."

Pier sat by the phone and debated on whether or not she should call Kyle. But what would she say? *Are you having sex with Monica or did you at one time?* That would make her look like an insecure teenage girl. No matter what, she couldn't let what happened to her and

Eric roll over into the next relationship. That Monica chick though was really bugging her out.

She tried to put herself in Monica's shoes. If she had had a good friend who was a male, would she act as if they were more than friends if he decided to bring his woman around her?

"Probably," Pier mumbled to herself.

But then again if she was a true friend of this person, she would want him to be happy more than anything else and put her opinions of the person he chose to be with on the back burner and support him.

"I'm going to call," she said as she picked up the phone and dialed Kyle's number.

"Hello," a woman's voice answered.

"May I please speak to Kyle?" Pier knew it was Monica and tried to be polite.

"He's not available to come to the phone right now, he's asleep."

"Well, I'm sure he won't mind if you wake him, it's Pier."

"I know who this is. Hold on for a minute." Monica put down the phone. Pier could hear some moving in the background. Then she heard Monica say something. Her voice was muffled and she couldn't make out exactly what it was that she said. A few moments later she came back to the phone.

"Nope. He's not waking up. I tried shaking him, playing with his hair and calling his name and he didn't budge. Should I tell him that you called?" Monica asked with a smirk on her face.

"Yes, and tell him that we're on for tonight." Pier hung up the phone.

Pier was hot. She knew that Monica was being funny with what she said and was trying to get under her skin.

Well, Pier got under Monica's skin when she confirmed plans for that night that didn't exist.

Without delay, Pier called and made reservations at Delta's, a soul food restaurant that she frequented. When she got off of work, she went and picked up a little black dress so that when she walked up to Kyle's door Monica would be totally envious of her. With an ass like a rhinoceros she couldn't be anything else but jealous of Pier. As she approached Kyle's door, she could feel that someone's eyes were on her. Just as she went to ring the door bell, the front door opened.

"Hi, my dad is in the bedroom," Stacey said as she waved for Pier to come in.

"Could you tell him that I'm here sweetheart?"

"Yes," she said as she ran away. Not less than a minute later, Monica came out.

"He has to work tonight."

Pier didn't answer. Her mere presence made Pier feel so uncomfortable. She felt as though Monica knew or wanted to know Kyle's every move. Stacey ran back into the room.

"My daddy said that he will be right out."

"Thank you honey," Pier said as she smiled at the child.

Pier took a seat on the couch since Monica hadn't asked her to. Monica then came and sat across from her. The two of them stared at each other as if that would determine who won Kyle. Monica's Plain Jane look made Pier feel like she was Miss America and the way that Monica looked at her made her think that she felt the same way.

"Nice dress, Kyle's favorite color is red."

"Well black is mine, and it's his too. Maybe he hasn't shared that with you."

"Red and white now that I think about it," Monica teased.

"White or a washed up gray because they can look alike in a certain kind of light," Pier shot back.

"Kyle is a really good friend of mine. I love him dearly and don't want to see him hurt."

"Okay, and you're saying this to me because . . ." Pier immediately became offended.

"Because again, he's my friend and I want the best for him."

"Excuse me," Pier stood up and just as she did, Kyle walked into the room. He was dressed in his uniform and was on his way to work.

"Didn't you get my message?" Pier asked him.

"What message?"

"I told Monica," Pier pointed to her, "that we were on for tonight. I made reservations at Delta's and everything."

"Oh I must've forgotten, Kyle, I apologize," Monica said poutingly.

"Wow, umm Pier, I apologize too. I do have an hour before I have to be in, would you like to grab something to eat? We can take it back to the station."

"I would love to," Pier shot Monica a look and took Kyle's hand.

"Monica, make sure that Stacey's homework is done and that she's in bed early."

"No problem Kyle." Monica was fuming.

Kyle and Pier ordered from Clancy's and took the food to the station like Kyle had suggested. As he walked her through and to his office, his fellow officers made comments on how pretty she was. One even bowed as if they were royalty.

"Come on now," Kyle tried to be modest. His office was all the way in the back where they had complete privacy.

"You know I'm really trying to respect the fact that Monica is your housekeeper/babysitter or whatever, but I'm really getting tired of her acting like she's your woman. What is that all about?"

"I don't know Pier. She's a part of my life because she takes really good care of Stacey and Stacey loves her. I apologize for her behavior and will definitely speak to her about it. I won't have you feeling uncomfortable when you visit my house. Give me a kiss."

Pier leaned over and kissed him on the lips. He took her hand and put it on his thigh. She moved it up and found his hardness.

"Oh, I'm sorry. But after the other night, I just had to feel it again. Kyle, I've never felt that way before. You really did your thing."

"There's more where that came from."

"I'm sure there is." Pier pulled out their food and they ate and had idle chit chat. When they were finished, Kyle walked her out to her car and said goodnight.

"Maybe we can do this another night, like tomorrow night, your place?"

"I'd like that. I'm going to cook you some real food. And I'll invite Corrine, April and Renee." Pier smiled and smacked him on the butt. "Bye." She got in her car and drove off.

Pier set the table as Renee, Corrine and April drilled her. They were best friends, and they were stuck on how Kyle acted at his party. Pier was not the wild type. She didn't dress sexy on a regular basis but that night, she was showing off more of the goods than normal.

"Why are you wearing that top?" Corrine asked.

"Well, I'm feeling a little sexy tonight. Kyle will love it don't you think?"

They looked at her and none of them answered. All three of them looked at her like she was crazy.

"What?"

"All I'm saying is that you are acting real out there."

"Excuse me but aren't you the same people that said I needed to move on, get over Eric and that whole situation? I mean, why can't you guys be happy for me?" Pier went into the kitchen. Corrine followed her.

"Listen girl, we do want you to be happy but you have to admit, that was some weird mess going on at that party. Trust me, I'm down for new and exciting things but that was way too much for me."

"Exactly, for you. It wasn't as bad as you guys think. They *were* drinking and getting a little out of hand I will admit but I tell you what though, that Monica chick, that's a strange situation between her and Kyle." Just as she finished her statement the doorbell rang.

"Okay, there he is. We'll finish this conversation later. How do I look?"

"You look good girl." Corrine gave her sister a kiss on the cheek.

When Kyle walked in, Pier introduced him to Corrine, Renee and April again. He was over dressed and wore too much cologne. They sat at the table and Pier brought out the food. Macaroni and cheese, fried chicken, fresh collard greens, yams and corn bread. Since they missed out on Delta's, Pier figured she would give him some home cooked soul food. Kyle sat back while Pier served him. Renee stared then shot April a look. They both sucked their teeth and continued eating. Corrine looked at her sister like she had lost her damn mind.

"So ladies, how have you been? You hurried out of my party like bats out of hell. That's too bad because we had a really good time, didn't we baby?"

Pier nodded in agreement. Neither Renee, Corrine nor April said anything so Pier broke their silence.

"They had something else to do and needed to leave, right?" Pier hinted to any one of them who would listen, but again, none of them responded.

"Maybe next time you'll stay around a little longer. I guarantee you'll enjoy yourselves."

Kyle was not making a good impression with the girls. They were not feeling his arrogance and over confidence. As he lifted his cup to drink, his pinky was pointed up. The girls noticed that his hands were manicured. Kyle didn't mind the attention. In fact he loved the fact that Pier's girls couldn't keep their eyes off of him.

As they ate dinner, Corinne, April and Renee watched as Pier tended to Kyle's every need. When he reached for the bread, she stopped him and reached for him. When his glass was half empty, she got up and filled it. This was not the Pier that they knew. She was almost submissive without him even asking her to be, and his quietness told them that he expected her to be just that way.

"So tell us about yourself Kyle," Renee said.

"Well there isn't too much to know. I'm a captain at the department. I have about thirty men under me. I've received many commendations with respect to my efforts on the job and do many things for the community. In addition, I head the food drive every year during the holidays with the help of the local housing authority and well, that puts smiles on many faces. I'm a wonderful father to my beautiful daughter Stacey who is seven years old and I am recently divorced. Thank goodness, I have no baby momma drama and I have an awesome nanny who cares for my daughter while I'm working and she performs many duties so that my household can run smoothly. I've done security for many politicians who have visited from out of town. And when I was sergeant, I had the biggest bust in the history of the department."

"I'd say that's a lot to be proud of," Pier touched his shoulder.

"What do you do for fun?" Corrine asked.

"Who has time for fun?" He laughed. "Seriously, I love to entertain. You would've seen that if you didn't skip out on the party so soon. Maybe the next one, you'll stay longer. But come with an open mind or you won't fit in at all."

"Excuse me. And what do you mean by that?"

"I mean, you can't come up in there all high sidity thinking you're all that, turning up your nose because you see something that you're not used to seeing."

"I think you're out of line," April didn't hold her tongue. "Forgive us if we have a little class about us. That party that you had going on was nothing but a bunch of people getting their freak on with stanky chicks who had no respect for themselves."

He reached for something to drink. Pier was beside herself.

"April, he was just saying."

"Saying what Pier? We didn't like what we saw so we left. Last time I checked, it was a free country. Oh what he's going to do, arrest us?"

"You have some very interesting friends Pier. I think I've worn out my welcome. I'll be going now."

"No, wait Kyle. Thanks April!" Pier shot her a dirty

look as she ran after Kyle. He was about to walk out of the door when she caught up to him.

"Kyle, wait. They're just over protective. You understand, don't you?"

"No. I don't. In fact you don't need them to protect you. Not only are you a grown woman, you have me for that. I tell you what, you better get your girls under control or I can't see myself being around them. They hate me."

"No they don't. Give them a chance and trust me when you get to know them, they're a lot of fun."

"Well maybe, but I've had my fun for the night. Call me tomorrow."

Pier closed the door behind him. She leaned up against it and shook her head. Corrine, April and Renee knew how important this was to her and they ruined it. She went in and gave them a piece of her mind.

"I know you're not flexing on us over him," Corrine pointed towards the door.

"Where are your manners? I would never do that to you whether I liked your date or not. This is my home and you guys just cut up."

"I don't like him Pier. He is so not your type. The entire time all you did was make sure that he was straight. Not once did you ask us if we needed anything."

"So is that what this is about? I paid more attention to him than you. Give me a break."

"That's not what she's saying Pier," Renee interjected. "He is really arrogant and doesn't seem to be your type at all. Even at the party, he controlled your every move. And you know that's not how you roll."

"You guys were the ones who told me to go ahead and try this. Now that I did, you're giving me grief about it. Make up your damn minds already. See yourselves out please," Pier said as she walked away.

"I'm making a plate to go if you don't mind," April shouted out to her.

"Something about him doesn't sit right with me. I hope she knows what she's doing."

"Corinne, that's your sis and all but I'm not feeling this dude and honestly don't feel comfortable around him. Now I'm going to just grab me a plate too and roll on out."

When April and Renee left, Corrine cleaned up the dishes and put the leftovers in the kitchen. She also made herself a plate to go then put the food away. Just as she was about to leave she heard Pier's voice coming from the bedroom. She tiptoed against the wall and put her ear up against the door. Pier was crying.

"Kyle, please answer the phone. I'm sorry about them. They don't understand. Call me back please." She hung up the phone and called him back, but again, no answer.

Corrine softly knocked and entered her room. She came and sat beside Pier. Corrine hugged Pier as she let out a cry fueled by frustration and anger. She was frustrated that it was the beginning of her relationship with Kyle and everything that has happened so far has been negative for the most part. She wondered if this was a sign that the relationship wasn't going to work. She was angry because her girls and her sisters, the only people that she thought she could count on to have her back, were adding fuel to the fire with their outbursts towards Kyle.

"All I want is to be happy," Pier said as she sobbed with her face in her hands.

"And we want you to be happy Pier, but something about his personality doesn't sit right with me. Now you do what you want but I'm just telling you how I feel. And I feel that he's nothing but bad news. Look at you.

You're crying and you haven't been dating that long. If it's like this now, what do you think it will be months from now, a year from now? Just keep your eyes and ears open."

Pier continued to cry. She had no response for Corrine. All she wanted to do was talk to Kyle.

Chapter Nine

The next morning, Pier tried calling Kyle once again. All she kept getting was his answering machine at home and voicemail on his cell. On her way to work she took a drive by his house. His car wasn't outside so she went to the station. She walked in and asked for him. The officer sitting at the window excused himself. He returned and told her that Kyle had left about a half an hour ago. Unconcerned with being late for work, Pier drove back to Kyle's house and waited for him. About an hour later he drove up. She jumped out of the car and ran over to him. He got out of the car and reached for the groceries in the back seat.

"Can I help you with that?"

"What are you doing here?"

"I've been calling you all morning. Why haven't you answered my calls?"

"I was busy. I do run a police department."

"Didn't you see that I called?"

"Why are you here? If it's to aggravate me, leave. I'm too tired to do this with you right now." He grabbed a few bags, walked up the stairs to open the door and there stood Monica.

"Give them to me Kyle," she said as she stood there in her robe.

"Thanks. Is Stacey off to school?"

"Yes." Monica took the bags from Kyle as he went to get the rest from the car.

"What is up with that? You say that she's your nanny but she acts like she's your wife or something."

"You're trippin' Pier. I'm going inside." She followed him

"Kyle, we need to talk." Pier followed him into the kitchen. Monica had begun to put the groceries away. "In private please." He walked past her and into the bedroom.

"Tell me you're not still mad from last night."

"I don't appreciate how your friends treated me. I came as your guest and they treated me like dirt. I didn't treat them that way when they were guests in my home so yes, I'm still upset about that." He began to take off his clothes.

"Actually you did make a nasty comment to them by calling them his sidity. But that's neither here nor there. You're punishing me for something that I didn't do."

"They're your friends."

"Kyle, I'm sorry."

"Don't be. I will tell you this though, I will not be disrespected by anyone. I don't care where I am. You better tell your friends to get used to me or we can end this now. I don't have time for these kinds of games. Do you know how many women want me? Please. They're dying for me to be available again."

"Don't say that Kyle. You know I don't want to break up. It won't happen again. I promise."

"You promise," he laughed. "And you don't want to

break up. You want me or do you need me?" He moved closer to her.

"I need you. I want you too."

"Do you love me?"

"Yes."

"Prove it."

Pier stared him in the eyes and knew that he was serious. He wanted her to prove that she loved him and wanted to stay with him. She began to caress his back and rub his arms. She lightly kissed his nipples through his tee shirt and squeezed his butt. He didn't respond to any of her touches.

"Tell me how to show you."

He took her by the back of the head and kissed her. Then he pushed her down onto her knees. Pier felt demeaned but she did want to be with him and if he wanted her to suck his dick to prove it, then that's what she was going to do.

The sex they had afterwards made it all worth the while to Pier. Kyle had her flipped over all kinds of ways. He sexed her from behind, on her side, on his dresser and against his wall. They ended up lying in the bed, satisfied and watching television. As Pier lay next to him, thoughts of Monica clouded her good mood. She couldn't understand how she stayed there and how Kyle pretty much let her have the run of the house. She had to let him know that just like he wanted to be respected, so did she and that would mean that if they were going to make a go at this relationship, he needed to let Monica know that she was going to be there more frequently if not every day and that she needed to show her just as much respect as she showed him.

"Kyle, we need to talk about Monica."

"What about her?"

"Just as you want my friends to respect your position

in my life, I feel the same when it comes to her. I think that if we're going to be together, she needs to stop with the dirty looks and the smart remarks. And I would like to formally meet your daughter."

He looked over at her.

"Okay. That's no problem."

At that second, there was a knock at the door. Monica asked if he needed anything. She was about to run out to do errands and wouldn't be back for a while. Kyle got out of the bed and put on his robe. Pier grabbed her clothes and went into the bathroom.

"We'll address the issue now. Get dressed and meet me in the kitchen."

When Pier came into the kitchen, Monica was sitting opposite Kyle at the kitchen nook. She didn't seem too happy and didn't make eye contact with Pier.

"Monica is aware of the concerns that you have. In speaking with her she understands that you and I are together and she is to treat you with nothing but respect. If there is any instance where you feel that she's not, you let me know and it will be addressed. If we can't come to a resolution, she will be relieved of her duties here."

"I apologize for being nasty to you," Monica said still without looking at Pier.

"I accept. We can start new." Pier stuck out her hand and Monica reluctantly shook it. When Pier tried to release her handshake, Monica held on and tightened up her grip. Pier looked her in the eyes. Kyle left the room. Monica tightened her grasp of Pier's hand even more and didn't blink an eye when she spoke. Once Kyle was completely out sight, Monica added one last thing.

"Don't take my kindness for weakness. I'm doing this for Kyle. I don't give a damn about you!"

* * *

"That bitch said it, yes she did."

"And what did Kyle have to say about it?" Corrine asked.

"He went off when I told him but what does that really mean, you know? I was two seconds from putting my foot up her ass and you know I don't normally talk like this but she's getting on my last nerve."

"So what are you going to do? It seems like you like Kyle and you want to continue to see him, but how can you do that when she's constantly throwing daggers? You're better than I am," Corrine stated.

"I'm gonna get her by herself and we're going to resolve this thing once and for all. Kyle said that he wanted to be respected by my friends and I demand the same respect from her. After all, I may end up being the woman of the house."

"Oh you really see you guys hooking up like that?"

"I'm keeping my options open." Pier sat down. "I really think that they did have something going on. She wouldn't say that he was hers first but she basically told me that I'd have to share him if we did get together."

"Girl, I would've cold capped her in her mouth. I know you're trying to be better than that, but I can see where this whole thing is going. She's going to push you and you're going to loose it."

Corrine was right. Monica had already gotten on Pier's bad side. And even with that, Pier was willing to put all that aside and try and be cordial, for Stacey's sake more than anybody else's. But it was obvious that Monica was determined to make Pier's stay minimal or miserable. Either way Pier knew that Monica was going to be a problem and that she had a fight on her hands.

That evening the girls decided to have a movie night at April and Renee's house because they had the ultimate DVD collection. They cooked finger foods and bought a few bottles of wine and were all dressed in sweats. They turned off their cell phones and relaxed uninterrupted. Two movies into the evening, Pier turned on her cell phone and found that she had several messages. She listened to him.

"Aww, Kyle is worried," she said as she listened to his first message. The second was from him too. He wanted to speak to her to make sure that she was okay. The third and fourth pretty much expressed the same concern but the fifth, sixth and seventh painted a different picture. He didn't ask her to call him back, he pretty much demanded and threatened that if she didn't, she would be sorry. She let the girls listen to the messages. All agreed that the messages made him seem controlling, even in the first few. Pier didn't see that. She saw that he cared about her and that he was overall concerned of her whereabouts.

"Okay, he's a whack job."

"You're funny Corrine," Pier laughed. "Don't hate because my man cares about me and wants to know that I'm safe. I like the feeling that someone cares about me. He called me not once, twice but seven times to see if I was okay. That's alright with me."

"I don't know about that Pier. That's a little much for me. Seven times, what do you think, Renee?" April turned off the television. The talk was about to get serious.

"I wouldn't like it. It's like I met this dude on a dating website. We talked for a few months and met up at Delta's one evening for dinner. In the beginning it was nice. We talked about things in general. Then he switched on me. He wanted me to meet his parents, children and family members. He started talking about moving closer to where I was and then mentioned marriage. All this inside of a few months and it's been how many weeks with you and Kyle. No. It's way too fast and if you all into it, you *would* be telling him that you're okay with his approach."

"And what do you think Corrine and April? I mean let me have it because I'm feeling him. I'm not thinking about Monica, she'll have to be okay. But you're on the outside looking in and I really want to know how you feel."

"Personally, like I said before, I don't think he's your type," Corrine began. "He's bigger than the guys you usually date. I mean look at his job, he's in control of an entire police force. What if you guys do hook up and you move in, do you think that he can leave the need for control at work? It's his way or no way because he is the boss. Are you willing to let him be the boss and are you willing to shut up and listen?"

"That's a good question Corrine." April poured something to drink. "Granted the time we've spent with him hasn't been great, I see all the things that Renee and Corrine pointed out. And to top it off, he seems like he requires a lot of attention, like he needs to be the center of attention. Not for nothing, we had a dinner at your house. The way he came in, you would've thought we were at a black tie affair and the way he smelled was a bit much too. He seems to overdo it with everything and that's a sure sign of someone who is trying to compensate for something."

"Well it sure ain't the Richard because he can lay it down," Pier bragged.

"Okay, that's too much information and besides, that doesn't mean that he's good with everything else. Do you see any of the things that we are saying to you in him? I know you're emotionally involved but be honest with yourself. And do you know why he and his wife got a divorce?"

"Yes, she was a trip. She cheated on him and everything. Then had the nerve to start dating the scum bags that he locked up. Trifling thing."

"Just remember Pier that there are two sides to every story."

"What are you saying April? You're overreacting."

"Just what I said, there's his side, her side, and somewhere in the middle lies the truth. Don't be so blind so soon Pier. That can get you into a lot of trouble."

"And don't be so judgmental either, April."

"I don't think that she's being judgmental Pier," Corrine disagreed. "I think that we're all concerned. I know we encouraged you to give this a try, but we don't want you to lose sight of what you want while making sure that he's good, because then you'll be repeating that cycle and end up alone in the end again. That's all we're trying to say. Be open-minded, take mental notes and don't settle."

The girls made a lot of sense, but Pier felt that they were being too harsh on Kyle. They didn't really know him. It seemed that everybody got off on the wrong foot and Pier needed to get them all on the same page. How she was going to do that was anybody's guess. Moments later her cell phone rang again. It was Kyle.

"Hey there handsome. I got your messages. I miss you too."

April rolled her eyes, Corrine and Renee shook their heads resorting to the notion that Pier was under Kyle's spell. They listened to her conversation and wondered how she got hooked on him as quickly as she did.

"Oh that's great," Pier continued.

Fifteen minutes later she hung up with Kyle. Apparently, he was going to receive yet another official commendation for his efforts on the job. He invited her to the ceremony that would be held the following weekend and it was going to be a formal affair.

"And afterwards he's having a party. He invited you guys to come if you want."

"No thank you," April gave her decision.

"Nah, girl, something about him doesn't sit right with me," Renee said.

"Me either but I'll go to be there for you. If it was anything like the last party, you need me there."

"It's a key party. It should be a lot of fun."

"What's a key party?" April asked.

I don't know. He said that he would tell me later but that I would enjoy it.

All week Corrine and Pier went shopping for dresses to wear for the special occasion. They picked up shoes and accessories as well. They made appointments to get their hair done that Friday at a salon in Red Bank and were ready at 6:30 sharp that evening.

When he arrived at Pier's house, Pier and Corrine were surprised to see that he drove a convertible BMW and it was only a two seater. Pier felt awkward and initially told Kyle that she would drive with Corrine and meet him there but he vehemently objected. Corrine, against Pier's suggestion to meet her at the ceremony, gave Kyle a piece of her mind.

"Wait, you invite us to come to your ceremony, offer to pick us up and you show up here in a car that only has two seats? What kind of mess is that? Can you be serious?"

"I didn't know you were going to ride with us Corrine. When I offered to pick Pier up, I didn't even know that she was going to bring you with her. So I guess we're both surprised."

Corrine looked at her sister. For a moment she thought that Pier was going to tell Kyle that she'd meet him there, but when she opened her mouth and asked her sister to drive herself and handed her the directions that she had printed out to the hall, Corrine flipped her wig.

"What, you're not going to leave with him and make me drive by myself."

"Corrine, it's not that serious. We'll meet you there. He came all this way and I'm not going to make him drive by himself. I am his date after all."

"You know what, you gone! This dude has got you wrapped around his little finger. Tell you what, you go and enjoy your man's ceremony. I'm going home." Corrine handed Pier the directions.

"We don't need those. I know the way," Kyle said.

Corrine shot Kyle a look, rolled her eyes at her sister, got in her car and left. She was fuming and convinced that Kyle had Pier seeing stars with his big head in the middle of them. *Is she that desperate,* Corrine thought as she fought back the tears of being put on the back burner by her sister and her best friend, for a man she hardly knew? She thought she was doing her sister a favor by going with her, but obviously Pier didn't need Corrine.

When Kyle and Pier walked into the room, everyone there stopped eating and drinking and applauded. Kyle took a few steps ahead of Pier and accepted his welcome, then began to work the room as if he were running for president. Pier walked over to a woman who was handing out table assignments and asked for Kyle's table. The woman regretfully informed her that Kyle would be sitting on the panel and she would have to find a seat wherever there was room. Pier went to object to Kyle but he was pulled away by another woman. Rather than make a scene, she found one of the unreserved tables and took a seat. It was in the back of the room.

As the room filled to its capacity, Pier ended up sitting with the dispatchers that worked with Kyle, four men and one woman. The men engaged in manly talk while the one woman sat back, listened and drank. They were one step above the scum of the earth but Pier thought she'd better make some kind of conversation otherwise she'd be in for a long night.

"So is this an annual event," she asked.

"Yes. It would be nice though if someone else other than Kyle was appreciated. There are over a hundred other officers who do a damn good job and he's the only one they give shine to. Humph, guess it pays to sleep your way up to the top."

"What do you mean by that?" This woman had Pier's undivided attention.

"I mean that when Kyle came here, he was a rookie just like the rest of them. But since he's got that look about him and is the biggest Uncle Tom in Monmouth County, he quickly moved up the ladder. And not only from eating crow but from screwing everything he could. Little do they know, he liked to swing at the bottom of the todem pole too. All the women had some piece of Kyle at one time or another."

Pier sat in silence. She tried to look over at Kyle but he was surrounded by people in suits and full uniforms. He was shaking hands with one, hugging another and was

Stephanie Johnson

the center of everyone's attention. Pier didn't want to let on that she was there for Kyle to avoid being laughed at and since the woman was offering all the information on him, she continued to prod and listen and got angrier by the minute.

"Wow, that's too wild. What about his wife? Does she know that he's been around like that?"

"Are you kidding me? How do you think they hooked up? She used to work here before they got married. And she should've known that it wasn't going to work when everybody told her how they were with him. He's such a dog. A dressed up, dirty, nasty pissy dog!"

Pier was floored. If it didn't show on her face, this woman that she talked to was blind. She began to sweat and felt her heart begin to race. The woman continued.

"Girl, I got smart quick. When he beat my ass for not conforming to his retarded sexual fantasies of him dominating me, I was done. Put me in the hospital with one broken rib and knocked out my front teeth. See." The woman pushed her bridge out with her tongue.

"Oh my gosh, are you serious?"

"She's a lying thing," one of the men who sat at the table slurred. "When he didn't want her, she made all of these accusations about him and put the man through all of this court mumbo jumbo. It was a shame what she did to him. You ought to be ashamed of yourself."

Pier stared at the man.

"Shut up because nobody asked you. How did this happen then? Like I have nothing else to do but blame him for this."

"You don't have anything, that's the point. You just as broke as the rest of us and all you were trying to do was sue the department and Kyle so that you can have a little something. Trifling hoe."

The woman took the rest of her drink, got up from

the table and removed herself, but before she did, she shared one more thing with Pier.

"Rumor has it that he had a child out of wedlock and that's why he got divorced. Don't let him see you, you're just his type. Will charm the pants off of you so I suggest you get your date and keep him by your side so that he knows you're not available. But then knowing Kyle, he'll peep you on the low and find a way to get to you. And you'll fall for him just like the rest f us."

"Ah don't listen to her," the one man continued.

Pier got up from the table and went outside to get some air. Everything that the woman said ran through her mind, from him being a philanderer to him having a child out of wedlock. Kyle didn't seem like that type of man to her. Everybody has a past and that was his past. She wasn't going to let that stop her from being in a relationship with him. So what he was a little controlling. He was good to her and she was in love.

She went back inside and took her seat. The ceremony had begun. All of the formalities took about an hour, then Kyle was presented with his award. He thanked the mayor, his superiors at the job, his fellow co-workers and said a few other words. The food was buffet-style and they began calling the tables, starting with Kyle's. It took everything for Pier not to walk up to him and be by his side. Between the anxiety that she was feeling and the want to be next to him, she needed to get herself a drink so that she could calm down. The bar was a few feet away from where she sat. She ordered a Hennessey on the rocks with lots of lime. Her appetite was gone and she couldn't wait to get Kyle alone. Her dilemma was that she didn't know if she should mention to him what was said or not. It bothered her to know all of that about him and she didn't know if she could hide her feelings long enough for him not to notice.

The ceremony was over by 11:00. On the ride home, Pier was quiet. Kyle didn't seem to notice that anything was wrong. All he did was talk about how he got his commendation and all the other accolades that he'd gotten in the past, and if he continued doing what he did, what his future would hold. Not once did he ask her if she had a good time or why she was so quiet, so Pier just sat and listened. Her mind drifted to her sister and how she didn't really miss anything that evening. Had she been there when that woman said all of those things about Kyle, Pier would've never heard the end of it.

They pulled up to Pier's place.

"Well thanks for coming out and supporting me. I really appreciate it." Kyle spoke to her as if she was a voter whose vote put him over the top, not the woman he wanted to be with. She looked over at him and smiled.

"I had a really nice time. I see that you have a lot of people who think highly of you."

"Yes."

"And some who don't." Pier opened the car door. He grabbed her by the arm and pulled her back into the car.

"What do you mean by that?"

"Just that a woman who sat at my table had some not-so-nice things to say about you. I imagine it was jealously."

"There are a lot of people who are jealous and I'm sure you added to that."

"How so?"

"Everybody wants a pretty girl on their arm."

"Kyle that is so superficial. I'm more than just a pretty girl. And I didn't tell anyone that I was with you so that can't be the reason why they would say those things. I know that people can be cruel, but I heard some pretty messed up things."

"Sure you are and you should know that you can't be-lieve everything you hear, good or bad. Give me a kiss and I'll see you tomorrow at the key party?"

"What is a key party Kyle?"

"It's when people get together, drop their keys in a bowl. Whomever's keys you pull out, you sleep with."

"Yeah right." She didn't believe him.

She leaned over and let him kiss her. Now Pier was feeling even more uneasy. What did he mean good or bad? So she should pay no attention to all of the nice things that his friends said about him at his party. She was uneasy as she got out of the car. She closed the door behind her and stood there. Before driving off, Kyle pulled out his cell phone and made a call. He rolled down the window.

"Good night baby," he said to Pier then he spoke into the phone.

"Monica?"

Chapter Ten

The following evening was Kyle's key party. Pier didn't even bother asking her sister or Renee and April to come because they just weren't feeling Kyle at all. It really hurt her that they felt thay way but everybody was entitled to their own opinion and she respected that. She just hoped that they respected her decision to be with Kyle as well. When she got to Kyle's, cars were lined on both sides of the street. There had to be over fifty people there. As she walked in, there was a huge bowl that held everybody's keys. Pier thought that made sense if his guests were going to be drinking but that's not what Kyle said the party was about. She kept her keys with her. She said hello to those who sat in the living room as she made her way to the kitchen where it seemed everyone was hanging out. There was light music and food everywhere. It was wall to wall with people. Pier saw Kyle and walked over to him. He saw her coming and held out his arms. She walked right into a big hug. He hugged her so tight that it sent chills up her back. Kyle's kiss on her head made her smile.

"That was nice," she patted him on the stomach.

"It's good to see my baby here."

"Thanks, just what I needed." Together Kyle and Pier walked about the house, hand in hand, as they laughed with the guests. Monica was amongst them and was pleasant for the first time. Pier welcomed it given what she felt last night. She wasn't up to another night of hearing or seeing anything negative.

In each room there were different adult games from trivia to sexual. Everyone played all the games but were mostly excited about the theme of the party itself. Pier had to ask.

"Really, what is a key party?"

"Baby, I told you. It's when everyone puts their keys in a big bowl and at the end of the night, they grab a set of keys."

"Okay. And what again?" Pier wanted to be sure she heard him correctly the night before.

"And whom evers keys you grab is the person who you have to sleep with. Not everyone will do it but a lot will. Did you put your keys in the bowl?"

"No. And I'm not going to."

"Why not?"

"I'm not sleeping with anyone but you!"

"It's all in fun Pier."

"That's plain old nasty. I don't know these folks and there are too many diseases out there. I can't believe that you would have a party like that. And I thought your last one was weird. This is way over the top."

"Don't be so judgmental Pier. I'm not doing it. I just happen to have friends who are into that kinky stuff and I like to entertain to the fullest in my home, to the liking of my guests. What is so wrong about that?"

"Nothing as long as you're not sleeping with any-one."

* * *

Kyle reached into his pocket and pulled out his keys. Pier followed as he went into the kitchen and got a little bowl. He asked Pier for her keys and put them both in the bowl.

"Now take a set of keys." Pier grabbed his and he grabbed hers. She smiled at his little game and couldn't wait to get him in the bedroom.

At the end of the night, those who wanted to play the key game did. They didn't stay at Kyle's house. They actually went home with whom ever's keys they picked up and had sex. Pier couldn't believe the amount of people who played the game. These were respected pillars of the community and they were screwing other people's spouses or mates. When everyone left, Kyle shook his keys. Pier looked over and made eye contact. He licked his lips and signaled with his head for her to head to his bedroom.

"Get her ready for me. I'm going to straighten up a little bit."

Pier walked toward the bedroom and on her way, she noticed that Monica's light was on. She hesitated as she thought about knocking and having light conversation with her. The entire evening, Monica was respectful of Pier and she wanted to thank her for a nice spread. Pier figured one nice gesture deserved another, so she knocked.

"Who is it?"

"Monica, it's Pier. Can I come in?"

"Go away."

Pier stepped back. Then she heard Monica begin to cry. She tried to open the door, but it was locked, She knocked again.

"Monica, are you okay? What's the matter?" Pier was genuinely concerned.

The door opened. Monica turned and went to sit on

her bed. Pier entered the room and closed the door behind her. She sat beside Monica. The nice thing to do would be to comfort her in some way but Pier wasn't feeling that close to her. Instead, she leaned over and waited for Monica to say something.

"Monica, why are you crying like this?"

"Because I cooked all of this food and not once did Kyle, or you for that matter, invite me to come and hang out with the rest of the company. Ungrateful, he's so ungrateful."

"Wait Monica, I think we need to have a talk. I need some clarification on some things and maybe I can clear up some things for you as well. You are the nanny, right?"

"Yes, I am the nanny, but I'm more than a nanny. I take care of this house, Stacey, Kyle and now will be making sure you're taken care of too. So don't minimize my job Pier!"

"I wasn't minimizing anything. It seems to me that you take things too personal and too far. Since the first day I stepped in this house, you were rude to me as if I pissed on your fire hydrant. I'm sorry if my being here upsets you but I'm with Kyle and will be spending a lot of time here. I just want to be able to get along, that's all."

"You think you know everything." Monica got up and opened her bedroom door.

Pier got up and walked towards Monica.

"I know enough to say this. I'm sorry that you can't handle the fact that Kyle and I are together. I'm sorry that no matter how I try to be nice to you, you reject my efforts. I mean no harm to you but I will not allow you to push me away. Have a good night."

Monica slammed the door behind Pier as she went on to Kyle's bedroom where she found him stretched across the bed. She told him about her conversation with Monica.

"Kyle she really needs to go. I only work part time and can take care of Stacey. I'll be home when she gets out of school. If we are going to try and make this relationship work, she needs to go. If she can't accept that it just won't work."

"I hear you and you're right."

Kyle got up and left the bedroom. Moments later, Pier could hear him and Monica arguing. She wanted to be with Kyle and Monica wasn't going to stop her from doing so.

"You bastard!" Monica yelled. "Who took care of your daughter when you worked all those crazy hours? Who cooked for your spoiled ass? What other woman do you think will put up with your bullshit? She'll see, you wait. She will see what a motherfucker you are. I'll be back for my things."

Monica stormed out of the front door and Kyle returned to the bedroom.

"What happened?"

"I told her that if she couldn't respect our relationship then she had to go. I'm not going to have her making your life miserable because then, I'll be miserable. Monica has been this way for some time but since I hadn't found a woman that I wanted to be with as much as I do you, I didn't let it bother me to the point where I wanted her to leave. Enough is enough though and her time has ran out. As for you, I think that you should meet Stacey as soon as possible. How does tomorrow sound?"

"That sounds great Kyle. You know I am not a trouble maker, but Monica was a little too much for me to handle. I'm sure she's been good to you and your daughter, but I'm here now," She said giving him a hug.

While in his arms she felt so safe and secure. Almost

like nothing could touch her. She thought of the things that were said about Kyle at the ceremony and none of it mattered anymore. Kyle redeemed himself by letting Monica go. To Pier, that said that he wanted to be committed to her and that she had a secure position in his life. Shortly after they went to bed.

The following morning, Kyle had taken both Pier and Stacey out to breakfast so that they could formally meet. Initially Stacey was apprehensive, but after Pier broke the ice and began talking about her school and what activities she liked Stacey was okay. She liked Pier. The only thing she wanted to know was where her mother went and when she was coming back.

Chapter Eleven

Although Kyle didn't answer Stacey's question, Pier found it odd that she would ask about her mother at that particular time. Maybe she told her that she wasn't going to be home or something, but Pier was definitely lost. Kyle seemed unconcerned with her inquiry and completely brushed it off by offering to take her to the arcade. Pier chose to stay at the house and call Corrine, April and Renee.

"He sure did put her ass right out. They were arguing and everything. I was glad that he stood up for me."

"It seems strange that they would argue about it like you say they did. Sounds like she was emotionally charged and who gets so emotional over a job? A nanny job at that."

"Corrine, I kind of understand why she would. I mean she's been around Stacey for some time now and I'm sure they have developed a relationship so she'll miss her. And Stacey will miss Monica. But she was crazy and we both couldn't be in that house."

"That's all well and good but like Corrine and I said, if

she was tripping like they had more than an employer/ employee, relationship," April reminded Pier.

"Look at him, who wouldn't want to have him to themselves in a sexual manner. He's fine, has a good job, has everything going for him, and no baby momma drama. Please, it's gonna be okay."

"How do you know how her mother is going to react to Monica being fired? If Monica gets to her first, then you can best believe that she's going to fill her head with all kinds of lies so be ready."

"Kyle paid Monica, not Stacey's mother, so I don't think either one of us is worried about that. Stacey is seven years old. She doesn't have the capability to judge."

"No, but adults do have the capability to brainwash and cloud the minds of a child in a heartbeat. And you know an angry and rebellious child can be worse that an angry adult. You are at a risk of her playing Kyle against you and that will definitely create friction between you two," Renee warned.

"Again, if that happens then I'll just deal with it. I'm going to put my best effort into this relationship and I think he will too."

"Well as long as you're happy."

"I am happy." Pier didn't want to tell her sister and girlfriends what she was told about Kyle. They already weren't feeling him and that would seal the deal. Whether it was the truth or not, they would never bless her relationship with him. And besides, she chose to throw caution to the wind and not allow it to have any bearing on the growth of their relationship.

Pier got off the phone and sat still for a moment. She looked around the house. She could definitely see her-self making this her home. Beautiful furniture, a gorgeous kitchen, two large bathrooms, and huge bedrooms. She had to give it to Monica, she kept the house immaculate. There wasn't going to be too much for Pier to do to add her flavor to it. Some new curtains and pillows for the couch, new sheets for Kyle's and her bed would do the trick. She would run it by him and get his okay to make some changes first. While Kyle was still out with his daughter, Pier went around the house and looked in the closets, drawers, and the kitchen cabinets. Everything was in order. Nothing was out of place.

"Anal how all of this stuff is so situated," she said. She went downstairs into the basement, which was partially done, and again boxes were labeled on shelves and nothing was out of order. Architectural plans were stapled to one of the walls which indicated that Kyle had intentions of finishing the basement.

Kyle returned home with Stacey just before dark. By then Pier had gone out and gotten dinner. She figured every child loved chicken fingers so she ordered out from Applebee's. They sat and had dinner while Stacey talked about her day with her father. Her eyes lit up with adoration when she looked at him. That made Pier smile.

"Ms. Pier, my mommy will be home soon."

Pier looked at Kyle and waited for an explanation to Stacey's comment. He offered none so she spoke to Stacey directly.

"And where is your mommy, Stacey?" Pier dared to ask.

That got Kyle's attention. He stopped eating and looked at Pier. Her eyes met his but as he stared harder and didn't look away, she softened her gaze and asked nothing else.

"Stacey, finish up so that you can get your bath."

While Kyle got Stacey settled for the night, Pier cleaned

up after them. She put away the leftovers, cleaned the table, threw the napkins in the laundry and wiped down the kitchen counters. Kyle returned to the kitchen.

"I put some water on for tea."

Before she could ask if he wanted some, Kyle had a few choice words for Pier.

"Pier, don't you ever question Stacey about anything. She's a child and will say things out of the blue. I didn't appreciate you asking her about her mother. If you have any questions you ask me, not her."

"I didn't mean anything by it Kyle. It was the second time that she made reference to her mother not being here or coming back. I mean, obviously she wants her mother here."

"Her mother and I are not together. She may have a hard time understanding that and may get confused sometimes. She's a little girl and you have no right to question her about anything."

"I'm sorry. It won't happen again," she said as she got a mug out of the cabinet. Kyle walked over to the refrigerator and saw Pier's list of changes that she wanted to run by him.

"What's this?"

"Well," she came and stood next to him, "these are things that I would like to add my personal touch to, but only if you don't mind. I gathered you like your house a certain way and that's okay but you know, I'd like to bring a little bit of me in here."

"Oh really. You're a trip. Bold I might add. I don't mind if you change anything just don't touch Stacey's room unless she asks you specifically and leave Monica's room. I'm going to call her and arrange for her to come and pick up the rest of her things."

"Can't we just mail them to her?"

"No. I fired her, that's enough don't you think? Pier

listen, I know you guys didn't get along but Monica has been a part of Stacey's life for some time now. Are you going to have a problem with her being in her life at a distance? I just can't see completely removing her. Besides, unless you're going to quit your part time job and be here all of the time to make sure that things continue to run as smoothly as they have been, we may need her to pitch in."

"Oh no, no we don't need her. So you're saying that you want me to quit my job and be a full time what? Live-in girlfriend? Because I don't really like depending on people and if I do that, I'll be dependent on you for everything."

"And what's wrong with that? You know I can provide for you. All you would need to do is maintain the house and make sure that Stacey was taken care of. She is my main concern."

"I can do that, but what happens when I need money to buy something, anything? Are you going to give me a hard time if I take money out of the account? That's another thing, who's account will I be using yours, mine or ours?"

"I understand and don't have a problem having a joint account. It should be like that since you will be my live-in woman, lover, and provider for my child." He moved closer to her. "You would like that right? I mean you love being around me don't you? Hate leaving me when you have to, right? Then move in and let's do this."

"Are you serious Kyle? I mean really serious? I can't be played with. I've been through enough games and yes, I love being around you, miss you when you're not near me. And last but certainly not least would love to go to sleep next to you every night and wake up smelling like you every morning. Yes, let's do this."

* * *

During the next couple of weeks, Pier moved the rest of her things into Kyle's house. She gave up her lease and sold her furniture. Kyle helped her clean up the place before she handed in the keys so that she could get part of her security back.

"But you don't need it. I don't see why we have to clean this place. Let them keep the security and hire someone to do it."

"No baby, I want to do it and thanks for helping me." She planted a big kiss on his lips.

As he continued to grunt, Pier came across some pictures that she had stuffed in the back of the closet. They were pictures of her and Eric. She stared at them and remembered the day she moved in with him, then tore them up. She knew that her relationship with Kyle was different. When they were finished, they threw out the garbage and dropped off the keys to the rental office. Now all she had to do was call her sister, April and Renee and tell them the good news.

"You are about the most naïve chick I know. Why would you move in with him?" Corrine wasn't happy at all.

"Because we're together Corrine, that's why. I'm always here, I met his daughter and everything is going great. You're just still upset over what happened and I wish you would let it go. It was a huge misunderstanding and he later apologized just so you know."

"Pier, you're the only one that has to accept him and if that's what you want to do then okay. I don't have to. He's an arrogant man and personally I don't see you guys lasting. Just be careful."

"Well, first impressions are lasting impressions. But like Pier said, Corrine, it was a misunderstanding and if she's happy then we should support her," Renee added.

"I agree with Renee," April said.

"Thanks y'all and I know Corrine will come around. I'm her sister, right girl?"

"You'll always be my sister and I'll always love you."

It had been a month since Pier moved in completely with Kyle. She had quit her job and became a full-time stepmother to Stacey. Kyle had his shift switched to day-time so that he could be there with Stacey and Pier. He had arranged for Monica to come and get the rest of her things the following weekend while both he and Pier were home. He also allowed her a few minutes with Stacey, which he later regretted because Stacey didn't want her to go.

"Why Daddy?"

"Let me just take her for an hour or so after school. This is a major change for her Kyle. You have no idea what you're doing," Monica pleaded.

"I don't think so Monica. I think it's best this way. Come on Stacey. You can call her and if you want to visit it will be here, with Pier and I. Do you have a problem with that?"

"No. I would appreciate that Kyle." Monica would do anything to be in his presence and Kyle knew that he would want Monica at some point as well and if Pier got comfortable with her being there every now and then, he and Monica would eventually get back to the way things were between them.

Kyle had missed not being able to slip into Monica's room and have sex with her. It was a part of his everyday routine. Since he hadn't had a steady girlfriend and she was down for whatever he wanted, he loved being with her. Nothing mattered to her as long as she could be with him. Kyle knew that she was in love with him, but he wasn't in love with her. He used her for sex and in return she took care of his house and his daughter. She'd never betrayed him by telling what they did, because she knew he would kick her to the curb without hesitation. He would just need to get her warmed up to the idea that he and Pier were going to be together and warn her not to start any problems. As far as Pier was concerned, she didn't need to know what happened in the past between him and Monica. All he needed to do was keep what was going to happen between him and Monica a secret from that day forward.

When Monica pulled up, Pier tightened her jaw. She anticipated that Monica would say something that would cause her to go off but she promised Kyle that she would be the bigger person and avoid any confrontation. Kyle was in the back and Stacey was in her bedroom playing with her dolls. She watched as Monica straightened herself up before getting out of the car. She put on lipstick and tossed her hair. As she walked up to the door, Pier tried to relax then opened the door.

"Hello Monica, come on in." Pier held the door open for her. She and Kyle had taken the liberty of packing her things in boxes so that the furthest she would have to go was the living room. They sat in the far corner. Pier pointed to them.

"We thought we would save you some time and have your things ready." An unintentional smile came across Pier's face. Monica didn't say anything. She heard Stacey talking in her room and proceeded to walk to her. Pier stepped in front of her and pointed to her boxes again.

"There are your things Monica. There is nothing left in your old room, so there is no need for you to roam around the house."

"I wasn't going to roam. I was going to see Stacey."

"Stacey is having her quiet time."

"I'm sure Kyle won't mind. He is here, I saw his car outside. Kyle!" she yelled.

"Excuse me but he's busy right now. I suggest that you get your things and be on your way. I will sit whatever you can't carry on the porch, if that will help."

"You bitch. You think that you've won. I will always be a part of this family whether you like it or not. Hell, I may even be at your wedding. That is if Kyle ever decides to settle down and stop playing house."

"Get out!"

Monica went and stacked one box on top of another. There were three boxes left. When Monica took those two to her car, Pier literally threw the other boxes on the front yard leaving some of Monica's belongings scattered on the grass. Monica looked back at her and laughed. As she picked up her things, she continued to laugh in Pier's face. Kyle had heard everything and when he knew that Monica was outside the house, he looked out his bedroom window. He made movements to get her attention and when he did, he blew her a kiss and mouthed, I love you.

"You could never be me, girl. All of the sisters that came through here had a short stay and you're no different. Society says that you're what he should have but honey child as you and your home girls say in the hood, there are some things that will never change. And Stacey, she loves me. She'll want me to come and pick her up or better yet, she'll want me back and Kyle does anything for his little girl. So I wouldn't get too comfortable. You may have to share him with more than just one."

"You're one sick bitch and in need of counseling. Don't you ever step another foot on my property or 'honey child' and as we say in the hood, 'you will get that big ass torn out the frame'."

"Umm yes, I like that. I will have to come back some-time next week because I ordered some things and they're being delivered here. Can someone call me when they arrive, please? Thanks and smooches!"

Pier's blood was boiling. Monica had pushed every button there was and to throw Stacey in there was just wrong. She had to calm down before Kyle saw that she was upset. Pier didn't want to share what had happened with him. She was the woman of the house and she han-dled it. She sat at the table for a moment. She heard a shuffle and there stood Stacey.
"Hey honey, what's up?"
"What was that noise?"
"It was nothing, just some people passing and making a whole bunch of noise. Want some cookies?" Stacey nodded yes.

Later that evening, Kyle called Monica on the tele-phone.
"You look great. Did you loose a few pounds?" He asked as he walked through her door.
"What do you think? I've only been stressed the hell out. How could you do that to me? You promised that I would always have a home there. And what about Stacey? How is she supposed to get along?"
"She'll be okay and yes, I did promise you that but I never thought I would find someone like Pier. Someone who would leave everything for me and be there for me no matter what. You always gave me problems and I told you before that would bite you in the ass in the end. I suggest you calm down. Hell I'm still paying you to keep your mouth shut, what else do you want?"
"You know what I want. I need to see you Kyle."
"Not tonight."

"Then when you bastard?"

"Monica, chill. I'm telling you, you better get it under control. I want to get my household settled. It's only been a month and things have been going great. Then you show up here acting a fool. You can't just get your things, you have to run that big ass mouth of yours. Now I have to put out the fire. So you have to wait." Kyle raised his voice enough for Pier to hear.

Pier looked up. "I'll be right back baby," she said to Stacey as she walked to the bedroom.

"Kyle who are you talking to like that?"

"Hold on," he said to Monica, who was getting satisfaction just being on the phone while he lied to Pier. He didn't even cover the telephone.

"There was a huge arrest at the job. I'll need to go in because these guys can't seem to handle it."

"Okay. Will you be long?"

"No, it should only take a minute."

"See you in a few baby," Monica yelled at the top of her lungs hoping that Pier heard her.

Chapter Twelve

Kyle had gone out to see Monica the next day. He knew that if he gave into her and had sex with her, she wouldn't stop until Pier had had enough and left. The fact of the matter was that Monica wasn't stable. She couldn't control her emotions and was depressed most of the time. She knew a lot about the things that Kyle had done and gotten himself into and he wanted to keep those things away from Pier.

When he got there, she was dressed in a night gown and had two drinks ready. As hard as it was for Kyle to reject the pussy, he did. He told her that they couldn't be together like that anymore. For how long, he didn't know. He shared with her that if everything went well with Pier he would be asking her to marry him. He needed to do that for his daughter. She deserved a stable home and a stable mother figure. Naturally, Monica didn't like what Kyle said and began to trip, but he stood his ground.

She cried, drank, cried and drank until she drank herself to sleep. He put her in the bed and made sure that she was okay. All in all, he did care for her but she was too out there for him. He realized then that he should have never allowed her to come and be his daughter's nanny. When he tried to break up with her she pulled the same stunt and to keep her from blabbing her mouth to his superiors, he let her move in, paid her as if she was legitimately working for him and gave him sex anytime of the day or night.

When she was sound asleep, he looked over her place. She had pictures of him all over. Some from when he got awards, some when he was on calls, some when he was relaxing in his bedroom and she even had some of Stacey. That didn't surprise him as much as her having pictures of him because he knew that she loved Stacey, but he had no idea that she was that crazy over him. He grabbed all of the pictures and put them in a bag. He let himself out and took a ride to the recycling depot a few neighborhoods away. He flashed his badge and they let him in with no question. He looked for the incineration batch of debris and tossed the bag of pictures in it. At that moment, he thought that he had successfully communicated to Monica his intentions and what he expected of her. He had no worries and was convinced that there would be no more problems from Monica.

When Monica woke up the following afternoon and realized that her some of her things were missing, she called the police. What Kyle didn't realize was that she wasn't asleep at all. She knew he was there taking the pictures and even got up at one point and saw him put some in a bag. She quickly got back in the bed and began to devise her plan.

The officers came and questioned her. They asked if she had any known enemies and the first person that she said was Pier. Knowing that the routine was to dust for finger prints, since Kyle had been in her place before, his would be all over. Once they found his prints and ran them, they would bring him in for questioning. That would be sure to light a flame under Pier's ass.

Hours later the director of the police department knocked at Pier and Kyle's door. She was asleep and thought that she was dreaming, but when the knocks got harder and they began calling Kyle's name, she jumped out of bed and went to answer the door. Kyle wasn't home.

"Yes, can I help you?"

"Yes, is the captain around?"

"No he's not, but I'm sure you can reach him on his cell phone. Is there something wrong?"

"No. Please if you see him, have him contact me at the department. It's of a business nature." He handed her his card.

"Of course I will."

As soon as they left, Pier called Kyle on his cell phone. She told him to call his job because they needed to speak with him.

"About what?"

"I don't know Kyle. They said it was of a business nature. Is everything okay?"

"Yes, why wouldn't it be? It's probably about the case from last night. I'll shoot down there now to see what's up. I'll be home for dinner."

Immediately after he hung up the phone with Pier, Kyle went down to the station. He knocked on the director's door. As he entered, there was the detective from Internal Affairs. They had taken the report that Monica had filed and placed it in front of him. Everyone knew of their indiscretions when she worked as a dispatcher, despite their attempts to keep it under cover, and were not happy at the potential outcome of this incident.

"What's this?"

"Read it Kyle. She alleges that you came into her apartment unbeknownst to her and removed all of her photographs. I thought you had this under control Kyle. We don't want any domestic anything with you and this woman. You were warned that she was 50 cards short of a deck, but you insisted on continuing the relationship."

"First of all, what I do on my personal time is my business. I'm no different than you guys when it comes to this stuff, so don't act like the shoe has never been on the other foot. Did you go to my house?"

"You know we did. We had to, it's procedure. Don't worry we didn't disclose any information. Is that your new girlfriend?"

"Yes."

"I assume that this is what this report is all about?"

"Yes it is." Kyle felt comfortable saying that because Monica couldn't prove that he was in her apartment without her consent.

"Figures."

"Exactly. She's upset because I went over there as I did many nights before last night to break it off with her. I told her that I couldn't see her on an intimate level anymore and she said that she would get me back. Well I guess this is how she meant."

"It's nothing, but we don't want it to turn into something so be as nice as you can be to her so that she doesn't make any waves for you here at the job or at home. That new one, she's a hottie."

"Right. Watch yourself and I take it you will take care of this." He tossed the report back onto the desk.

"Of course, but type up your version of the story so

that it can be properly noted for each side. Consider it closed."

Kyle went to his office and typed up his account of what happened. When he was finished, he went for a ride. Monica knew that she could do anything. She could throw a bitch fit, break up dishes, ruin his clothes, but under no circumstances was she to go to his job and cause him to be embarrassed. He had a reputation to protect and she knew how he felt about what the public and his coworkers thought about him. She also knew that he wouldn't risk his being fired behind anybody or anything so she was safe from any retaliation from him, but from Pier that was a different story.

Chapter Thirteen

"That bitch did what? What were you doing at her house anyway? I thought we understood that she was out of our lives."

"Pier before you came along, I did go over there and I'm sorry to say that I did make the mistake of sleeping with her a few times and baby, I am so sorry."

"What? Damn it, Kyle you said that you never slept with her. You lied!"

"No, not really. Before she came here to work for me we did fool around but I promise once she came to be Stacey's nanny, all of that stopped. I swear I didn't sleep with her after I hired her."

"Kyle, you lied! I can't believe this. How can I trust you now? I mean, damn!"

"Baby," he got up and wrapped his arms around her. Her back was to him. "I promise you that I haven't been with her in a long time. And I didn't start having problems from her until you came around. When she figured out that you were going to become a permanent part of my life, she lost it. She felt that I thought she wasn't good enough for me. And she wasn't. Any woman who lets a man get in her pants the first night that they meet, baby, that's not the woman for me. She's nothing to me. You have to believe me."

"How can I believe you Kyle when I asked you straight out if you two had anything going on and you said no? Whether it was the past or the present, you had a relationship with her. I really wish you would've told me."

"I just didn't see what difference it would've made knowing who I dealt with in the past. I didn't ask you who you dealt with, did I?"

"No you didn't, but you don't have some brother knocking at your door, disrespecting you because he's my ex do you? And had you asked me anything, I would've told you. I can't handle the lies Kyle. I just won't deal with that."

"Baby, I apologize again." He turned her to face him. "I'm sorry that I didn't tell you about her and I'm sorry that you're so upset. I can't stand her and she knew what she was doing. She just wanted to cause problems between us. Don't let her. If I knew anybody that could handle her, man, her ass would be handled before the sun rose, stupid bitch."

"Well I'm telling you this right now, I'm not going to let her mess up what we are trying to do. We can't blend as a family with all of these outside influences. She has one more time before I put my two cents into it and handle her myself and Kyle, no more lies. It will be the death of us."

"You got it baby. I love that about you. You give people the benefit of the doubt. Think our children will have that character trait?"

"What, who said anything about children?"

"You don't want to have my baby? Hmm?"

"Not without being married I don't."

"Married, I see." He let her go and turned away. He turned right back around and got on one knee. Pier's eyes widened. Her stomach began to get jittery. He took her hand and looked her in the eyes.

"Marry me baby. Be my wife."

"Kyle, what?" She began to cry.

"Marry me. Let's do this right from the door. Never mind anybody else and what they think. I want you to be mine."

"This is so sudden and with everything that's going on, Kyle, I just don't know."

"What do you mean you don't know? You love me don't you?"

"Yes."

"You want me to be with you right?"

"Yes baby I do."

"Then what's stopping us? You can't put a time on when people fall in love. Love is love and isn't something that we can control. Let's show the world that we're in love. MARRY ME!"

"Yes. Yes, Kyle I'll marry you."

They went ring shopping and settled on a princess cut with baguettes along each side. While they were at it they picked up their wedding bands as well. They were simple gold bands. Pier immediately started thinking of how many people she would invite to their wedding. She knew that it wouldn't be a lot on her behalf because she didn't have many friends. Her sister, April, Renee and a few of her co-workers would pretty much be it. Kyle on the other hand would probably have tons of people there.

"I would say 50-75 people. But I think that people spend way too much money on weddings when they can use it for other things. Know what I mean?"

"I understand but this is my wedding. I want the whole kit and caboodle."

"And you can have that. Go get your dress, hair and nails done and be the princess that you want to be. All I'm saying is that we don't want to go over board. Did you tell your sister and two side kicks yet?"

"No and be quiet. Those are my girls. Despite everything, they've stuck by me through thick and thin and I love them."

"Did you tell them what's been going on with Monica? They'll really hate me then."

"They don't hate you Kyle. It's the same thing with how you said Monica was with you, protective. I've never slept with them though."

"Oh, so it's like that. You're gonna bring that up."

"Chill out baby I've forgiven you. I'm marrying you aren't I?"

Pier was worried about how the girls were going to respond to her telling them that she was going to marry Kyle, but she had to break the news to them sooner or later. Maybe if they were in public, the blow wouldn't be so hard.

"Are you out your damn mind?" Corrine shouted in the middle of the restaurant. Clancy's served the best clams which were Corrine's favorite. Pier had hoped if she fed her clams, she would be a little more accepting of Kyle becoming her brother-in-law.

"Congratulations," April said and took a sip of her drink.

"Are you pregnant?" Renee asked.

"No. I'm not pregnant and thank you April. Listen, I love him and I'm going to marry him. I appreciate all of your concern, but I'm good. We talked about everything that may have been an issue before he asked me to marry him. It's okay."

"What do you mean issue? Are you talking about that Monica girl? Was there actually something between the two of them?"

"A long time ago they used to 'have sex'. She was just a bootie call."

April shook her head. Renee continued eating without lifting her head up while Corrine grew another head.

"You mean to tell me that he slept with this woman then hired her as his nanny? Does that sound right to you? How do you know that he's not still sleeping with this woman or when he actually stopped sleeping with her? He's lied from the door and you expect him to stop lying because you guys get married? I'm sorry babe but this is a mistake. I love you, you're my sister but I can't give you my blessing. You're walking straight down the aisle to hell."

"You know hearing that from anybody else, I probably wouldn't feel like my ankles were hanging off of a dime but hearing my own sister say that she won't stand by my side on my wedding day hurts my heart like you wouldn't believe. I know people have their opinions but if you were happy with someone I would stand by your side even if there were things that could possibly be an issue in the future. So you're saying that you won't be in my wedding? Is that what I'm hearing?"

"Pier, I want you to be happy but I just don't see that you will be. Maybe because I'm on the outside looking in and I see what you maybe don't or choose not to see. Either way, I feel like you're making a mistake."

"She's your sister. You should support her no matter what she decides and you should be there should it not work or whatever," April said.

Pier began to cry. Her feelings were hurt and she felt alone even with the little support she was getting from April and Renee. Corrine was her best friend, they were tight and to not have her support hurt her heart.

"I'll do it. I'm sorry if I came off judgmental and unsupportive. I will be by your side." Corrine had a huge lump in her throat. To see her sister cry made her want to cry herself but also she saw her sister crying through this farce of a marriage and ultimately being hurt beyond belief.

The following weeks consisted of looking for a wedding dress, dresses for the girls to wear, a florist, a place to have the ceremony, a caterer, and gifts for the wedding party. Favors, a DJ and a dress for Stacey, who would be the flower girl, were also among the items on the shopping list. Pier had already decided that she wanted to go to Disney for their honeymoon since she had never been there.

The wedding date was set for mid November, less than two months away. Pier had to get a move on things and get deposits paid as soon as she could. Kyle gave her a fairly generous budget, nothing outrageous and so far everything that she planned fell within it. The one thing that she would spare no costs was on her and Stacey's dress. She wanted them to be almost identical, with the color and sequence on Pier's being the difference.

She did her shopping during school hours so that she wouldn't interfere with the arranged schedule to pick up Stacey. By the time the day was done, she was exhausted. Kyle had been working as much overtime as he could to make sure that they had enough money for the wedding and he was pleasantly surprised when Pier showed him quotes and receipts for things that she had already confirmed and paid for.

"Baby I am having such a time planning this wedding. And I understand that you have to work and can't be there with me, but I know you're there in spirit. I do miss not seeing you as much. Good thing it's right around the corner. We'll be husband and wife."

"Umm hmm baby. That's true." He smiled at her.

"What's the matter baby?"

"Nothing Pier, I'm just tired."

The reality was that Kyle, while working over time doing patrol, was making his way over to Monica's place. In his eyes, it was simple damage control. If he had to keep her happy by sleeping with her once or twice a week, then that's what he was going to do. She could ruin what he had with Pier or better yet, his job and cause him to loose his pension and all the years that he put in. It simply wasn't worth pissing Monica off.

Did he feel guilty? No. This was how he'd always been. The women in his past came across finding out that he was with other women the same way that Pier did. His first wife found out about Monica and left. The women in between never made it past the first time they were together. They too wanted Monica out but none of them were Kyle's example of a wife so they left when he wouldn't dismiss Monica. Those are a few reasons why Monica felt like she always had an in with Kyle.

Despite his infidelity with Monica, Kyle really did love Pier. She was innocent to him, not pure, but trainable to his liking, and in some ways, submissive. Now that she didn't work, he could mold her and teach her how she should be while giving her financial security and sealing his marriage on the notion that she could never leave and if she did, she would do so with what she came there with, nothing.

* * *

Kyle also spoke to his lawyer friend. She advised him to devise a prenuptial to protect himself. Although he felt that he had it all covered, a prenuptial wasn't a bad thing to have should all else fail.

"I don't see why we need a prenuptial. To me it's like you're thinking that we're doomed already, planning our divorce before we even get married."

"That's not it. Look I built this house. If I lose it to you because we break up, what will that leave Stacey?" Kyle said concerned.

"I understand that but who have you been talking to?" Pier asked as she sat up in the bed. Kyle stood and leaned on the dresser.

"Nobody. I've just have had a lot of time to think and Pier, I'm putting everything on the line here. I have a lot to lose if things don't work out."

"I can't believe you're saying this to me. Do you not want to get married anymore, Kyle?"

"Yes, I do want to get married. I'm just trying to protect my interest."

"Kyle if you want me to sign one then I will. I'm hurt that you would even think that I would want to take this house from you should we not work out. This has me feeling like you have doubts, but if my signing will make you feel better, then where is it?"

"I didn't have anything drawn up yet. I wanted to talk to you about it. I don't think you would ever, but I guess you never know. We'll revisit it again some other time."

Kyle got in the bed and watched television. Pier turned over and turned off her light. She wanted him to think she was asleep. She was bothered by Kyle's request and wanted to drill him more about it but if she did, he would think that he had grounds to make such a request. If she came off as concerned with having one, he may push for one. But then she thought that may not be so bad because if he wanted to protect what he came into the relationship with, she could protect what she came into it with as well. She turned back over.

"Kyle, like I said, I understand where you may be concerned about loosing everything. But I can lose everything too. I may not have come into this situation with material assets, but I did come into it with honesty and an open heart. I've never lied to you or been with anyone since we've been together. So if you want a prenuptial then I want to add a clause in it."

"What would you want added if we decide to do one?"

"If you cheat, I get what's due to me. No questions asked."

Kyle never thought that Pier would come up with such a rebuttal. She made sense though and that made him think twice about it. If Monica came out of the woodwork about him, Pier could possibly be living in this house and he would be in somebody's apartment.

"You know I'm sorry if I made you feel uncomfortable by my request. Let's drop it. I was being silly by mentioning it. You've been nothing but supportive and accepting of me and my daughter."

"Okay baby. I just want to cover all bases. Speaking of which, did you decide who you wanted in the wedding as groomsmen? All you need is three."

"Yeah, I asked three of my co-workers. I assume you'll have the three stooges right."

Pier slanted her eyes. "Who else would I have? Yes."

"All they need to know is where to get the tuxedos."

Pier jumped out of the bed and reached in her purse for a card that she had picked up while shopping.

"I checked the prices and they're within budget so

there should be no problems. All they have to do is show up. They can manage that right?"

"Yes. Please make it as simple as possible. What are the colors?"

"I chose red."

"Red? Ugh, but whatever."

"It'll be nice. You'll see. The tuxedos look sharp with red cummerbunds. You too, I've seen the groom tuxedo and baby you're going to look fine. Makes me want to jump you right here, right now." She sat on top of him, pulled his robe open and put his nipple in her mouth. Her warm lips covered it and she gently sucked while she rubbed his member. The phone rang but neither of them answered. Surely it wasn't for Pier and the job could wait.

He rolled Pier over onto her back and took off her clothes. Then he went between her legs and tasted her. She opened up to him and let him lick her inner thighs, belly button and back down to her clit. Just as they were about to make love, there was a tiny knock at the door.

"Stacey?" Kyle asked.

"Mommy's on the phone."

Kyle jumped up and grabbed his robe. He stepped out of the room and closed the door behind him. He picked Stacey up and took the phone from her.

"Hold on." He placed the phone on the table in the hallway then he put Stacey back in the bed.

"Good night baby. Daddy will see you in the morning." He closed her door, grabbed the phone and went into the kitchen.

"Hello," he whispered.

"Just a couple of weeks and you'll be a married man," Monica taunted.

"Why are you calling this late? I told you this afternoon that I had to chill. Things are winding down and you need to be patient."

"I know, just wanted to say good night."

"Good night!"

"Tell my little angel I said sweet dreams."

Monica not being there seemed to be causing more problems for Kyle than he anticipated. Stacey was asking for her and missed being with her everyday. He knew that once she really got to know Pier she would love her as well, but she wanted Monica. He also knew that he couldn't hide who Stacey's mother was for much longer. He had no choice but to take her to see Monica and hopefully that would cut down on the inquiries from Stacey and minimize the chances of Monica dropping the bomb herself. He went back to bed.

"Who was that?"

"Nobody."

"How come I've never met Stacey's mother?"

Kyle didn't answer. He didn't want to have this conversation with Pier at that moment. He got nervous because Pier seemed like she wasn't going to let up until she got an answer.

"You would think that she would want to meet the woman who will be spending just as much, if not more, time with her daughter."

"What do you want me to say? Besides, that gives us time to mesh as a family. You will meet her in due time, trust me."

"I know I would want to know my child's stepmother."

"Let it go Pier."

Chapter Fourteen

On the day of the wedding, there were torrential downpours throughout the day. Pier and the girls, including Stacey, got dressed at her house. Kyle was supposed to get dressed at one of his friend's house. Everything was going well, with the exception of the weather, and Pier was happy. Her hair was perfect, her dress fit perfect, and all of the girls were beautiful. In less than an hour, she would be Mrs. Kyle Evans.

Pier looked at herself in the mirror. Just months ago, she thought she'd never find the man of her dreams, and there she was getting married.

"I'm just as shocked as you are," Corrine came up behind her and placed her hands on her shoulders. She leaned and whispered in her ear.

"You look absolutely stunning. I'm happy that you're happy Pier."

"Thank you Corrine."

The driver was outside. Renee and April grabbed Stacey and went into the car. Corrine helped Pier gather

her dress and made sure she got to the car without getting dirty.

Kyle sat at the table in Monica's kitchen. She sat across from him. Her eyes were red and puffy from crying. He'd been there all morning. They had sex and afterwards she flipped out on him.

Monica ranted and raved about how she was the better woman for him. She knew how to love him and knew everything about him. When Kyle didn't respond, she became physical. She tried to grab him around the neck, leaving scratch marks. The she slapped him. Kyle knew that if he hit her back, the first thing she would do was call his job. He was going to have a hard enough time trying to explain his condition to Pier. Being arrested was sure to call the wedding completely off.

"Kyle, I love you, you know I do. She doesn't love you like I do. You two hardly know each other. And how long do you think I'm going to let you keep Stacey away? You know you've completely disregarded our arrangement. You put me out for that bitch after everything I did for you!"

"Monica, it's only temporary. Let us get past the wedding. I already told you that you could keep Stacey while we go away on our honeymoon, right? That will be nice. You two can go shopping with the money I gave you and she'll be so excited to see you. She doesn't know that she will be staying with you, so it will be a big surprise to her."

"How much longer Kyle?"

"Not much. I'll tell Pier while we're away."

Monica helped Kyle get cleaned up as much as possible. She used some of her makeup to cover up the scratches. Luckily they were on the opposite side that

Pier would be standing on. He gave her a kiss and was on his way to the ceremony.

Pier waited until she was told that Kyle was there. She chose to get married and have the reception at the Hamilton Fire House. She and the girls decorated it beautifully.

The ceremony began and Pier was so nervous. Kyle stood with his best men next to him. First Corrine, then April and Renee, and finally Stacey walked down the aisle. When it was Pier's turn, she hesitated. She could see Kyle's face and it didn't look like the Kyle she had just saw yesterday. She walked slowly, giving him a smile to help ease what she thought were just cold feet, but he didn't smile back. He began to sweat and breathe heavily. She continued to smile even though seeing him like that gave her anxiety. When she reached him, the Justice of the Peace began. Pier looked into Kyle's eyes and he was able to force a smile.

"You are now pronounced man and wife. You may kiss your bride." Pier and Kyle kissed. She hugged him around the neck and didn't see the scratches. Kyle was put at ease and was able to relax for the reception.

Everyone was having a good time. The DJ did a good job and the food was delicious. Everybody danced the entire night. Pier threw her bouquet and a woman she didn't know caught it. Kyle threw the garder and one of his best men got it. All of the guests enjoyed themselves until it was time to go. After they bid their guests farewell, she wanted to tell Kyle her surprise for their honeymoon.

"Baby, I have a surprise for you." She handed him three tickets.

"Nice, where are we going?"

"We're going to Disney."

"Okay. But there are three tickets here." He frowned.

"Yes, I know. Stacey is going to go with us."

He paused. Kyle was shocked and it showed on his face. He began to sweat again because he had to break the news to Pier.

"Pier, Stacey isn't going on our honeymoon with us."

"What, why not? I thought it would be nice for the three of us to get away and have fun, Kyle. Please don't do this and besides where would she stay? We didn't make arrangements for her to stay with anyone while we were away."

"Can't one of your friends take her?" He wanted to use them first before he dropped the bomb that Monica would be taking her.

"No, they have to work. None of them are prepared to take care of her, make sure she gets to school and gets picked up on time. I was sure you would be excited about her coming."

"Well, I'm not. You should've discussed this with me before you made these plans. Let me make a few calls." He walked away and Pier slumped down in the chair. A few moments later he returned.

"I know you're not going to like this, but the only person that I can get to take her is Monica."

"What? No!" She jumped out of the chair.

"We don't have a choice. It's Monica or we can't go."

"Then we're not going. I won't leave Stacey with her unattended."

"Unattended? What is that supposed to mean? Monica has been around Stacey 'unattended' as you put it. She will stay with Monica and that's it."

"I'm not going Kyle. I don't understand why Stacey

can't go with us. And of all people, Monica? You know how I feel about her."

"Yes I do, but Stacey loves her. It will give her time to spend with her. And you are going. You spent my money to plan this, so yes you are going and you will have a nice time. You won't bring your pouting on our honeymoon and you will enjoy yourself. I'm serious Pier."

Kyle had just threatened her. Not only did he go against her and let Stacey stay with Monica, he basically told her that he made the decisions and that she had no choice but to accept it.

The flight to Disney for Pier was terrible. The entire time she fought back tears. If she cried or caused any undue embarrassment to Kyle, she was sure he would go off. When they landed, there was a car waiting to take them to their hotel. When they got to their hotel, Kyle seemed more agitated than he did earlier. He unpacked his clothes then ordered up a bottle of champagne. He knew he would need it. Pier took a shower and changed into more comfortable clothes. When room service arrived, they also had a delivery for Kyle and Pier. It was two dozen roses. The card congratulated them on their new union but wasn't signed.

Kyle poured them both a glass of champagne and proposed a toast.

"To us. Even though all of our days won't be the best, let us be happy." Pier lifted her glass without emotion.

"We need to talk Pier."

Pier got nervous. Kyle had a serious look on his face as he sat across from her. He didn't look her in the eyes when he told her what he needed to say.

"You are going to have to find a way to get along

with Monica. I know she's been very trying these last few months, but I can't remove her from Stacey's life."

"What the hell are you talking about?"

"What I'm talking about is that," he paused, "Monica is Stacey's mother."

"What? What Kyle? She's her fucking mother? What? How can that be?" She jumped up and threw her glass across the room.

"You better relax Pier. Sit down so we can discuss this."

"Fuck you!" She grabbed her bag that she hadn't yet unpacked, her purse, and tried to head out the door. Kyle jumped at her and tossed her on the bed, making her bags fall to the floor. He fell onto her and forced her hands above her head. She was breathing heavily and crying.

"You motherfucker. You lied to me from the door. I believed you and all you did was lie to me."

"I didn't lie. I just didn't tell you everything. I wanted to wait until it was the right time. Now, I'm going to let you go but you better not try anything. Understand?"

He slowly backed off of her. She continued to lay on the bed and didn't move. He began his confession.

"When I was married to my first wife, I cheated on her with Monica and she got pregnant. She threatened to go to my superiors and allege that I forced her to have sex with me. The only way she wouldn't do that is if I didn't object to her having the baby. Once she had the baby she demanded that I either allow her to come and be Stacey's nanny or she would take me to court for child support and then tell my superiors anyway. I couldn't let her ruin my career and everything that I worked so hard for, so I agreed. When I put her out, I was in breach of our agreement and she is now in a position to do what she threatened from the door."

With every word he spoke, Pier's heart fell apart. Once again, she allowed herself to be played by a man that she loved with all her heart. Everything that she thought they had built in their short period of time was a lie. He lied to her about everything.

"Pier, I'm sorry, I really am and I can't imagine how you are feeling. But I need you to be with me on this. You're my wife now."

"How could you do this to me?" She asked in a whisper as she lie still on the bed. He came and sat down next to her, his back facing her. He felt bad, but he couldn't allow Pier to go off the deep end because she now knew the secret that he'd kept quiet all this time and could ruin him just as badly as Monica.

"Pier, I didn't have a choice. I wasn't going to allow some whore to ruin my reputation at the job. A lot of people depend on me and trust me with things and I couldn't have my integrity questioned. I worked too hard to get where I am. I hope you understand."

"All I know Kyle is that I want to leave this place and go home. I want to have this marriage annulled and I want to be out of your life. You've done nothing but lie to me from day one and my simple ass believed everything you said, even though it was right in my face. Monica made it perfectly clear that she was involved with you the day I met her at your party, but you deflated her attempts to come between us with a straight face. I believed you. She tried on several occasions to tell me that she was more to you than you let on and I tossed it up to her being a jealous, overweight bitch who had a thing for you and was mad because you didn't give into her advances. This whole thing could've been avoided if I had only listened to her, not you."

Kyle quickly turned around and grabbed her by the neck.

"You will stay your ass here and be on our honeymoon. You are giving this thing too much energy and if you don't stop, you're going to regret it. Now, I apologized for having lied to you. Everything I said or didn't say wasn't a lie. I love you Pier, but I will not allow you to ruin me in the slightest fashion."

The entire honeymoon in Disney was the most depressing time in Pier's life. Kyle didn't leave her alone for one minute so she couldn't call Corrine. Then again, what would she say if she did? "You told me so. I should've listened to you". She couldn't tell then any of this and he knew it. He knew they didn't think he was good enough for her regardless of his status on the force. She couldn't wait to get home.

One by one, Pier ran down the list of mistakes she had made. She had given up everything to move into Kyle's house, which was still in his name entirely. When they got back, he acted as if nothing was wrong. He treated her as if she should be happy to be his wife and reassured her that everything would be okay. She on the other hand felt alone, scared and trapped in a situation that she didn't know how to get out of. She was curious though, how he kept his first wife quiet about his having a child outside of their marriage. She asked him.

"Why do you ask?"

"I just want to know."

"Well, I bought her out and in addition to that I agreed to pay her mortgage for a certain amount of time."

"So what you're saying is that you still have some

what of a relationship with this woman. You give her money monthly so that she will keep her mouth shut?"

"Yes, that is correct. Her life isn't bad, she's quite comfortable. Maybe you'll meet her one day."

"I'm going to bed."

"I'll be up in a minute baby. Be ready for me."

Chapter Fifteen

The following morning, Kyle went over to Monica's to pick up Stacey. When he was in front of the house, he called her on her cell phone and told her to open the door. Before he could step through it, Stacey ran into his arms. Monica stood behind and watched her daughter with her father. Kyle was so glad to see her and felt that a weight was lifted off of his shoulders since he told Pier the truth. After they hugged, Kyle sent Stacey to her room so that he could speak with Monica.

Monica had a different way about her too. She was more relaxed and happy that she didn't have to lie anymore. It killed her for Pier not to know that she was Stacey's mother. Now that Pier knew, it made Monica feel that she was on the same level as Pier, if not higher.

"How did she take it?"

"How do you think? She was rightfully upset. My telling her Monica doesn't give you the right to be there. It just opened the door for you and Stacey. She can spend time here now without there being any question. You and I are still what we were, nothing other than a sex thing. So don't get any bright ideas about starting any trouble. Don't think that just because the fact that we share a child is out in the open, that you can pull any kind of rank because I still run the show. I'll give you child support as agreed in the amount of your weekly salary and everything will be everything."

Monica didn't oppose, she was happy just having him around. Now he could come as he pleased and they could be together whenever they or he wanted. Pier would still be number two if to no one else but Stacey. When they were finished talking, Kyle and Monica had sex and Monica was finally satisfied.

When Kyle came home with Stacey, she was distant from Pier. She said hello but didn't offer any other greeting like a hug or a kiss. Kyle didn't press the issue because he knew that Pier was still pissed off and figured it would take a few days for her to get used to her new life. Pier on the other hand was a lost soul. She didn't know what to do next. It would be so easy to walk away but walk away to what or to whom? Then again, Kyle had already threatened her if she even thought about it. She basically had nothing and in order to save face, she would deal with the situation for the time being. As Kyle got Stacey settled and ready for bed, Pier decided that she needed some alone time and took a drive.

Emptiness overcame her. Pier was at a loss as to what her next move would be. She rode past Corrine's house and saw her car in the driveway but Pier couldn't bring herself to get out of the car and go up to the door. She even drove past April and Renee's place. They weren't home. She thought about calling them and seeing where they were because she really needed to talk to somebody. After driving for hours and stopping once for a cup of coffee, she returned home.

*   *   *

"Where were you?" Kyle asked. He was sitting in front of the television while Stacey was asleep on the couch.

"I went for a drive."

"Pier, come here. Have a seat." He pointed to the couch that Stacey was on. Pier went over, picked up Stacey's feet, sat down and placed them on her lap. Her little toes were so cute. She lightly touched them and thought how innocent she was in this whole thing. Resentment towards Stacey would be understandable, but how could Pier hold her responsible for her parents' actions?

"Kyle, I'm really not in the mood for any more of your lies. I have a lot of thinking to do and I just can't listen to you right now."

"You know, I don't see what the problem is. You had already accepted Stacey as my daughter but now that you found out that Monica is her mother, you can't accept it? Would it have been any different if her mother were someone else?"

"Yes it would've. The bottom line is that you lied. You didn't give me the option of deciding for myself if Monica would be someone that I would want to deal or have a relationship with. You decided for me through your lies and deceit." She rubbed Stacey's feet.

"Do you love her?" Pier asked.

"Of course I do. She's my daughter."

"Then why have you been bringing her up in such a dysfunctional manner? It didn't matter who it was that came into this home and became your wife. You would've done them the same way. I'm tired and I'm confused." Pier got up and left the room.

It was back to school for Stacey and work for Kyle. He remained on day shift so that he could monitor and make sure that everybody was getting acclimated to the new arrangements. Kyle had agreed to let Monica pick up Stacey from school, while Pier dropped her off. He was home by the time she got out, so Pier didn't have to deal with Monica directly.

When Monica dropped Stacey off, she wouldn't go up to the door. She would walk her up to the sidewalk and watch her go in and Kyle would meet her at the door. That was part of her agreement with Kyle. There was no need at that time for Pier and Monica to have any interactions, that would be a recipe for disaster.

Months went by and things appeared to have settled. After Pier dropped Stacey off at school, she would come back to the house and do what needed to be done. She fell into a depression that left her loosing weight and sleeping two hours each afternoon. She hardly spoke to her sister and girlfriends because between running errands for Kyle, taking care of the house, caring for Stacey and her depression, she had no time or energy. When she did find the time and energy to call them, she didn't speak on anything that was going on. As far as they were concerned, she was happily married.

Thanksgiving rolled around and Kyle had suggested that they have Thanksgiving dinner at their place and invite Corrine, April and Renee and a few of his friends. While Pier was against it, Kyle offered to invite them himself.

"Do what you want to do," was Pier's response.

It didn't matter what she wanted anyway. If he wanted them invited they were going to be invited. She ended up calling them because they would flat out decline his offer and she really needed her sister.

"Okay, yes we can do that. Is it okay with Kyle?" Corrine asked.

"It was actually his suggestion."

"Oh. I can come but I think April and Renee are going to see their parents down south."

"Alright. Just you being here is great. I really miss you."

"I miss you too. How is everything? Still feeling like a newlywed?"

Pier wanted to scream but she knew that Corrine would be upset and Pier just couldn't tell her what had been going on. Hearing her sister's voice lifted her spirits a little and she didn't want to ruin the moment.

"Yes, I'm good. We had a nice time in Florida. I'm just glad to be home."

"Okay, that doesn't sound like a newlywed to me. Are you sure that everything is okay?"

"Yes I'm sure. What's been going on with you?"

Pier talked with Corrine for some time never letting on about the problems she was having with Kyle. How would she be able to keep this from her when she saw her face to face? Corrine would most definitely notice the weight loss and Pier's ragged appearance. Pier knew she had to accept Monica and the role that she would play in her life because at the end of the day, she loved Kyle and wanted her marriage to work.

Thanksgiving eve, Pier cooked all evening. She prepared the side dishes and set the table so that she wouldn't have much to do other than run and pick up the dessert. Kyle helped a little by picking up around the house and running to the store if she needed something, and he did it without a fuss. Her thinking was that he was feeling a bit guilty about what he'd done and was trying to make it right. Even if it was just a little bit she appreciated it but still had no idea how she was going to make it through.

The following morning, she ran to the bakery and picked up the mini eclairs, cannoli's and cookies. On the way there, she saw Monica in passing. Her skin crawled and she got so angry that she had to pull over. She immediately got a headache and even cried a little. At least ten minutes passed before she got it together. When she returned to the house, Monica's car was parked out front. Pier grabbed the food and went into the house. There was Monica putting on Stacey's coat and getting ready to leave.

"What's going on? Where is she going?" Pier asked Kyle.

"She's going out with Monica for a little while. What time is dinner going to be ready so that she can have her back?"

"Five." Pier said and walked past Monica without saying a word to her or Stacey. She felt bad about not saying hi to Stacey but her emotions were so out of control. She couldn't hold Stacey responsible for this mess, she knew that, but that was easier said than done.

By noon Pier had decided that she wanted a glass of wine. Maybe that would settle her nerves a little bit. Corrine would be there at two to help her with the last minute things. The turkey was in the oven and was almost done. The house smelled like Thanksgiving dinner and usually a house was filled with family having a good time and enjoying each other's company. Her house was different. The issues in her life stood out like a piece of furniture. They were prominent and could not be denied. If she could get through this dinner without any upsetting moments, she would be thankful.

"Kyle," she called out to him.

He came from the back.

"Yes."

"Do you love me?"

"Yes, I love you. Why do ask?"

"No reason." She forced a smile and walked past him and into the bedroom. She was on the brink of tears and didn't want him to see her cry. He followed her and the moment she saw that he was in the room, she lost it. Kyle stood there and didn't say anything. She cried hysterically. Her stomach cramped and she squeezed her eyes tight and grinded her teeth hard. She was having a breakdown and in less than two hours, Corrine would be there, Stacey would be there and whomever Kyle invited over would be there and she would look a hot mess.

"Pier, I know you're still battling some feelings but you need to get it together. We're going to have company soon and I don't want them to see you like this. We can talk about it later," he said leaving the room. Pier went into the bathroom and applied a cold wash cloth to her eyes.

Corrine called Pier from the car to let her know that she was outside. Pier went to the door and opened it. By then the swelling of her eyes had gone down. She put on a little make up to hide the red blemishes on her cheeks hoping to pull off that nothing was bothering her.

"Hey you, what's happening?" Pier gave her sister a hug.

"Nothing much, glad to see you. Or what's left of you? Damn girl you lost weight."

"Yeah I've been walking and you know Stacey keeps me busy. I may not be working but I have a heck of a lot of things to do around here. Running here and running there, you know. I don't sit around the house and do nothing."

"Well you need to gain a little bit of that weight back. Too thin is not in honey."

They went into the house. Kyle was in the kitchen. He offered the both of them a glass of wine.

"Hi Kyle, sure." Corrine was caught off-guard by his kindness.

"What about you Pier, another?"

"Yes, thank you." Her tone was flat.

"Do you ladies mind if I join you?"

Pier looked at Corrine. She wanted to talk with her sister in private. Not that she was going to tell her what had been going on but just to catch up on old times. But it was obvious that Kyle was trying to be cordial and respectful of her sister so she didn't make a fuss about it. She patted the seat next to her and he sat down.

"So how have you been Corrine?"

"Good. I can't complain. How does it feel to be a newlywed?"

He laughed a little. "I love it. It's been a little trying but we love each other and everything will be okay. With the support of our family and friends everything will pan out. Speaking of which, I know we got started on the wrong foot, Corrine, but I want to be friends. I don't want to have any issues that will hinder the development of our sister-in-law, brother-in-law relationship. You are Pier's sister and I respect that. I want her to be happy and I want to be one of the people who brings happiness to her."

"Wow, Kyle. And yes, we did get off on the wrong foot. I want my sister to be happy too. All of that can be under the bridge as long as my sister is happy. Pier, are you happy?"

Stephanie Johnson

She nodded softly and looked over at Kyle. He winked at her.

"Well she's happy, so I'm happy. She's a little thin though. What have you been doing, not feeding her?" Corrine joked.

"No, that's not it at all. The blended family thing has been a bit of a transition for everyone. It's going to take some getting used to. In time everyone will find their place and be happy. Right baby?"

"Yes, you're right. Time. Speaking of which, what time are you expecting your guests and who did you invite anyway?"

"I invited the guys that were in the wedding. Before then, I didn't really associate with them outside of work but they are really cool and I figured it was about time that I let lose a little bit. You remember them right Corrine?"

"Yes, I do. They seemed to be nice guys. Where is Stacey?"

"She's out with the nanny. She took her out to keep her busy while Kyle and I got everything together."

Corrine looked at Pier then Kyle. It was really none of her business the extent of the relationship that they allowed Monica to have with Stacey. Clearly, Stacey was attached to this woman so she let it go.

"She will be coming for dinner right?"

"Yes of course." Pier sipped her wine. "She's a really sweet girl. I'm not used to being a step mom. In fact I don't really feel like a step mom. I don't know how I feel just yet. Like Kyle said, I have to find my space around here."

"You sure you're alright?" Corrine asked.

"Yes I'm good. Let's get it together. People will be coming soon."

* * *

As planned, everyone including Stacey was there at five. The table looked nice, the food smelled good and everybody was in good spirits. Even Pier and Kyle seemed to be getting along and interacting as if they had no prior problems between them. Pier put forth her best efforts because she was tired of feeling sad and depressed. She wanted this Thanksgiving to be a nice one, one that she would remember. She was in a new home, married and had a family now. This was what she had always wanted. Kyle also tried, because not only did he want his friends to feel welcomed and think that his house was full of love and family, but he didn't want Pier or Corrine to start acting up and causing any type of scene. It would go through the job like wild fire and that he didn't want.

Everybody ate and enjoyed each other's conversation. They told jokes, stories about their old relationships, good and bad, and talked about children. Corrine was really enjoying herself and Pier was happy about that. She thought she was opening Pandora's box by inviting her at the request of Kyle but it turned out okay. Kyle was pleasant and actually treated Pier like she was a queen in how he spoke to her and treated her in front of the company. She took that for what is was worth and treated him the same way just to keep it calm.

As the guests finished up their dinner, Kyle and Pier went into the living room, where Stacey was watching a movie. He felt that he could talk with her now that they were basically alone.

"Thank you Pier."

"For what Kyle?"

"For today. I know that the last couple of weeks have been difficult and I appreciate you handling things the way you are. Things will be different, I promise you.

Monica is Stacey's mother and neither one of us can change that. I've had a talk with her and she knows that you are the woman of this house and are to be treated as such."

"Kyle, I can adjust to her being around for Stacey's sake. As you said, she is her mother. But you're lies are so hurtful. I don't understand why you even felt the need to lie from the beginning. Everybody has a past so what did I say or do that made you think that you needed to lie or hide this from me? I feel awkward. I feel like she was privy to information and has one up on me. I know it sounds silly but that's how I feel. You need to make it right between us."

"I apologized Pier. What else can I do to get back in your good graces?"

"I don't know. I feel very alone and I shouldn't be feeling this way."

"If you can't tell me what it is that I can do to get on track then the only thing I can say is what I said before, time heals all wounds. Right sweetheart?" He tickled Stacey's neck.

He was right. He could care less that he didn't tell her in the beginning about Monica. He felt that because he told her, he was in the clear. If she wanted to harp on it and allow it to weigh her down, then that was on Pier. He didn't have a burden on his heart anymore and he felt that she shouldn't have one either.

Corrine came into the room to tell them she was leaving.

"Thanks so much for inviting me to dinner. I must say that I had a great time."

Kyle got up.

"Thanks for coming," he gave her a hug. "We have to get together again soon."

"Okay, that would be nice." Corrine looked at Pier as

if to say "what the . . ." Pier got up and gave her sister a hug and told her that she would call soon.

The other guests were also on their way out of the door and said their goodbye's at the same time.

"I'll walk you out," Kyle said to them as Corrine lagged behind.

"So, Pier, do you want to take Stacey out this weekend? I want to get better acquainted with my niece. Maybe a little shopping will do us all some good."

"Yes, that is a plan!"

Corrine left. Pier got Stacey up and ready for her bath.

"Bubbles or your rubber duckie?" She asked Stacey tossing one up in the air after the other.

"Bubbles," Stacey screamed with excitement. Pier ran the bath water and poured the bubbles while Stacey got undressed. Stacey jumped into the bath giggling with enthusiasm. Pier sat on the toilet and watched as she swished the water around to make the bubbles grow. She put her head under the running water and played. Pier stared at her. She was an adorable child and she alone would be a daily motivator for Pier to give this marriage her all.

Kyle came back into the house and called out for them.

"In the bathroom," Pier yelled back.

He came and stood at the door. He looked at his daughter then at Pier. He visualized Monica's face. It was twisted with anger and jealousy. Kyle knew he was dead wrong to keep the sexual part of their relationship going. Women like Monica, held on when they were in love with someone and couldn't have them. Even if he wanted to stop he couldn't because Monica would pull every one of her tricks out of the hat.

"When you're finished, meet me in the bedroom."

Pier let Stacey play for a little while longer. After fifteen minutes of splashing and pretending she was a submarine, Pier told her that she had to get out and get ready for bed. She promised her that if she did that without any problems, they would go shopping that weekend and that she could watch television for an hour. With no problems at all, Stacey got out of the tub, let Pier dry her off and willingly went into her bedroom to get her night clothes. Pier turned on the cartoon channel and tucked her in, then she met Kyle in the bedroom.

Chapter Sixteen

The love they made that morning was like it was the first time. Pier kept pushing thoughts of Kyle having ulterior motives out of her mind. She wanted to have a good day. Kyle was off to work. Stacey was still asleep so she made a pot of coffee and sat on the couch. Tons of talk shows and court television were on.

"You've seen one, you've seen them all," Pier said and turned the television to the music channel. The telephone rang. It was Monica and she wanted to know if Stacey was up.

"No, Monica she's not." There was silence. "Do you want me to have her call you?"

"Yes."

There was a click in Pier's ear. Pier just hung up the phone and sat back and tried to relax. Not ten minutes later did the phone rang again. It was Monica.

"I just got off of the phone with Kyle and he said for me to tell you to wake her up."

"Well you didn't have to call Kyle for that. If you wanted her up, all you had to do was ask me to get her up. Oh, but that would mean that you actually had to be civil. Hold on Monica, I will wake Stacey up."

Pier was angry and proud of herself at the same time. She was angry because Kyle should've told her not to call him with this type of nonsense. Was she going to call him every time she wanted something? She was proud because she handled herself very diplomatically and didn't go off on her. She actually felt good. Pier gently shook Stacey who was dead asleep and woke her up.

"Stacey baby, your mother is on the phone. Wake up honey." Stacey sat up in the bed and rubbed her eyes. Pier put the phone to her ear. She could hear Monica talking. She wanted to know if Stacey wanted to come over. Stacey shook her head yes but didn't say yes. Pier got on the phone.

"Monica, whatever you asked her she nodded yes."

"Then can you have her ready in an hour so I can come and pick her up?"

Pier took a deep breath. "Yes."

Stacey fell back into her bed. Pier hung up the phone and pulled her feet from out of the covers. She took off her socks and tickled her feet. A sleepy Stacey laughed and tried to pull her feet from Pier but she couldn't.

"Come on sleepy head, your mom will be here in an hour. What do you want for breakfast?"

"Eggs."

"Okay. Eggs it is." Pier went into Stacey's closet and pulled out a sweat suit. She lifted her out of the bed and gave her a kiss on the cheek. Stacey looked at Pier then smiled. She stood on her bed while Pier lifted off her nightgown and got her dressed. She jumped off of the bed, pulled out the socks she had on yesterday and started to put them on.

"Oh no little missy get clean ones." Stacey threw

them on the floor and went to her sock drawer and pulled out a clean pair.

"Grab your sneakers babe and I'll meet you in the kitchen."

Pier went into the kitchen and made Stacey's eggs. She poured her a glass of orange juice and fixed her place mat. Stacey came running and Pier helped her get onto the stool. She poured herself a fresh cup of coffee and sat with her as she ate. Her little heart-shaped lips were so cute. Her big brown eyes blinked every second, it seemed. It's no wonder her mother loved her so.

"So little momma, think we can be friends?"

She shook her head yes quickly.

"Cool, I'd like that very much! Now eat up so we can get your teeth brushed, your face washed and your hair combed."

Stacey stuffed the rest of her eggs in her mouth and washed it down with the orange juice. Pier looked at her and laughed. She told her to take her time before she choked. Stacey laughed and squirted orange juice on Pier. She immediately stopped laughing in fear of Pier's reaction. Pier stood still for a moment and watched Stacey's face fill with worry.

"It's okay honey. It was an accident." Pier assured Stacey.

She took her by the shoulders and explained to her that she would never yell at her. People make mistakes and it was okay. Then she thought about the whole situation with Kyle and wondered if she should be taking her own words of assurance to heart.

"Come on, let's get you ready for your mom."

An hour later on the dot Monica pulled up in front of the house. She beeped the horn. Pier put on Stacey's jacket and zipped it up. She gave her a kiss on the cheek and walked her out. Monica watched with disgust as

Pier, who was dressed in her robe, held Stacey's hand and brought her to the car. Pier stopped at the edge of the grass and waited for Monica to get out of the car and get her daughter. Stacey looked from one to the other. When Monica didn't move, Pier was left with no other choice but to put her in the car and buckle her up herself, so that's what she did. When she had Stacey in and was about to buckle her seatbelt, Monica lost it.

"Get the hell away from my car. You're not her mother."

Pier ignored her and continued to make sure Stacey was secure in the car.

"I said get away from my car." Monica got out. Pier quickly snapped the seatbelt in place and stood up so that her back was no longer to Monica.

"I was making sure that she was in her seatbelt. You have a nice day." With much control, Pier moved past Monica and started to walk back to the house. Her back was on fire from Monica's stare, but she kept on walking without turning around once. She walked in her house and closed the door behind her. Once inside, she fell against the door and let out a sigh. It was going to be work but she was determined to kill Monica with kindness.

Kyle came home around 3:30. Pier was folding towels in the bedroom. She heard him drop his keys and came out into the living room. She explained how the pick up went with Monica and then addressed the issue of her calling him instead of talking directly to her.

"I think you're expecting too much too soon. She feels threatened; why I don't know, and you need to keep that in mind. Remember, she lived here with Stacey all the time and to not be here anymore and have you re-place her, any woman would be upset."

"First of all she lived here under some bullshit. If you

two weren't together she shouldn't have been living here like that. You are part to blame for her thinking that she had that kind of clout and you said I replaced her?"

"You know what I mean. You're here and she's not."

"You know Kyle, I looked at Stacey today when we sat and she had breakfast. She's a beautiful girl, full of potential to have a loving heart. I want to be there for her. She and I had a great time this morning. The last thing that I want to do is step on Monica's toes. Since she would rather communicate through you instead of me, you need to communicate to her that I'm in no way shape or form trying to replace her, be in her shoes or whatever you want to call it. I'm good with my position in Stacey's life."

"I'm sure she'll be glad to know that. It's not going to make any difference whether I tell her that or not. She's just going to have to get used to it. Now speaking of which, did you cook?"

"No. There are so many leftovers I figured we'd have that."

"Okay. I'm going to go pick up Stacey."

Pier wanted to go but wanted him to ask her to go with him. She also wondered when he had arranged to pick Stacey up. For some reason she was under the impression that Monica would be dropping her back off at the house, but then she stopped herself. Kyle would have to have conversations with Monica that she wouldn't know about because they shared a child. He also never asked her to go with him.

Monica had her own Thanksgiving dinner spread waiting for Kyle when he got there. Stacey was putting forks out on the table when he walked in.

"This is nice."

"I wanted us to have our own Thanksgiving. Sit down and relax."

As soon as he did, Stacey jumped on his lap. He bounced her up and down and she was having a ball. He looked at Monica. He thought to himself "what was I thinking". She was available for sex anytime and that was all he wanted her for. How she maneuvered her way into his house and his life the way she did, he really didn't know. His intentions for going there were to talk with her and see where her head was. He already knew that she was crazy over him so he had to be careful in his approach on any subject relating to their relationship. She took his plate and filled it. He sat Stacey in the chair next to him.

"How was your visit baby?"

"Good. We played."

"Actually, we went to see a movie then came back here and got all of this ready just for you," Monica smiled.

"Thank you," he said directly to Stacey, not looking up at Monica.

"What's the matter?" She asked

"We need to talk. Maybe Stacey can go in her room."

Monica took Stacey and led her to her room where she pulled out crayons and a coloring book and began scribbling in it. She returned to the kitchen.

"About what Kyle?"

"Monica, you know when we first got together, how things were between us. Before you got pregnant with Stacey, you would come over to my place, I would sometimes come over to your place and every thing was good. We didn't have the kind of friction that we have between us now. I need to know how we can get back on that page because you can't keep doing Pier the way you have been. It will make everybody miserable, primarily me."

"So what you're saying is that I'm second to her."

"She's my wife."

"And I'm your daughter's mother."

"Yes, you are and I never tried to take that away from you. You were the one who made all of these threats of going to my boss. We could've raised Stacey in separate homes from the door but no, you had to have a brother by the balls."

"You didn't have to fall for it. So what, you had a baby with someone at your job. What, my being a dispatcher and you being in your position wouldn't look good to everyone? You're so worried about what people think. You should've thought about that when you had sex with me unprotected."

"You planned this didn't you? But you're right. I didn't wear protection. That's neither here nor there. Pier doesn't want to replace you in Stacey's life, she just wants peace in hers, no *ours*. So I'm asking you nicely to quit throwing daggers and work with me on this."

"What's in it for me?"

"Other that what you're currently getting from me, nothing. You're not going to get me for any more money. If you have to out me then do it. But no more money, you can believe that."

"That's not what I want."

She pointed to his crotch.

"That's what I want."

He was back to square one. Monica knew that he loved having sex with her. She wasn't the most attractive person and was heavy, but he loved to do it to her. And she knew this and used it to her advantage. He was always horny for her when he was around her. Pier didn't have that over her. He made love to her but he fucked Monica and she fucked him back. They're sex was nasty, some might say ungodly but it was how they were with each other. And so far, no other woman touched her when it came to the act. He loved her flesh.

Chapter Seventeen

Kyle knew that he had to save a little for Pier so he only came twice when he was with Monica. He washed up before he left her place so that he didn't have to do it when he got home. He put Stacey to bed. Pier was lying in the bed relaxing when he came in the bedroom. He took off his clothes and lay beside her. They looked into each other's eyes. She wanted to make love to her husband. He thought how he could muster up enough energy to bust one nut so that she wouldn't question him.

The only way that he could do that was to get a little freaky with her. He needed to talk dirty and get over excited so that he could perform. Their sex life wasn't bad but it was different from what he had with Monica. The sex he had with Monica was some old freaky mess. That was the difference between the two of them and was also the reason he kept having sex with Monica. He had to bring a little of that into the bed with Pier.

She leaned over onto his chest and softly kissed his nipples. She moved her hand slowly over his body and watched his body language at the same time. Despite the fact that he appeared to be very tense, she continued down his stomach and put her tongue in his belly button.

Kyle let out a heavy breath as he thought about how Monica had him in her mouth that day. The sheer excitement of possibly getting caught made her suck him harder. He remembered being so hard. He guided Pier's head to his dick with one hand and put it in her mouth with the other. He kept his hand on the back of her head as she slid up and down his shaft. He moaned.

"Damn, suck it."

Pier wasn't sure if he said something or if he was still moaning. He hardly ever verbalized any satisfaction when they had sex.

"Umm, that's it. Take all this." His mind went back to the same day when he fucked Monica while Pier took a shower. He had her ass in the air and was getting back shots in. He grinded his hips to the movements of her tongue against his penis.

"You like it baby?" Pier wanted to know how to please him.

"Yes but don't stop. Here take it." He shoved it back into her mouth. "Suck it slower." She did as he requested.

"Like this?"

"Be quiet, baby damn."

She sucked and did whatever he told her to do. She felt his hardness in the back of her throat. The head of his penis pulsated as if he were about to cum. If he had let her continue to suck it the way she was, he would've.

"I want you inside of me."

"Turn over," he ordered her.

Pier turned over onto her stomach and let him rub up against her ass. Then he pulled her up by the hips and spread her as wide as he could. He tried to simulate

Monica's ass but she was way bigger than Pier. So again, he imagined that he was fucking her that night she was half drunk and half asleep and gave it to Pier like he had never before.

All Pier could think was that he had to love her the way he was making her feel. Maybe he wasn't good at showing her on an every day basis how much he cared for her. Maybe he really was sorry for what he had put her through those last few months. Whatever it was that was bad between them he was making it right as he loved her that night.

The following morning, Kyle had already left when Pier woke up. That was the best sleep that she'd had in a long time. Her body was relaxed, her mind was on cloud nine and she had no frustrations. She got up and went to check on Stacey. The door was closed but she could hear Stacey talking. She lightly knocked on it then went in only to find Monica there straightening up Stacey's room. It appeared that she had folded the load of laundry that Pier had done the day before and was about to put Stacey in the bath.

"How did you get in here?"

"I called this morning and there wasn't any answer. So I called Kyle and he told me that if I wanted to see Stacey that you were home and to just come over. So that's what I did."

"Who let you in?"

"Well when no one answered the door after I knocked for ten minutes, I went to Stacey's window and threw tiny rocks until she came to it, saw me and let me in the front door."

Pier stood in utter silence. Her blood was boiling at that point. She pictured herself taking an ax and cutting that bitch's head off her shoulders. Thank goodness Stacey was busy dressing up her dolls to notice that Pier was on the verge of exploding.

"I need to see you in the kitchen Monica." Pier turned and walked out. A few moments later Monica joined Pier in the kitchen.

"Now you listen and you listen good. You will not come into this house uninvited. How and why you would involve Stacey in your ridiculous games I have no idea. If you haven't noticed or maybe you forgot, I'm Mrs. Kyle Evans and you will respect me as such."

"Please Pier. Whether you like it or not Kyle and I will be connected in a way that you will never. I have his daughter, his first child, and that gives me a little more leeway than the average ex-girlfriend."

"Ex-girlfriend, yeah right. You're a whore who happened to have enough screws to know that if you got pregnant, she would be financially secure for at least eighteen years. You don't intimidate me Monica. I've tried to be nothing but nice to you and that's it. Get out of my house and I will explain to Stacey why you had to leave so suddenly."

"She's my daughter and she's coming with me."

"Ah, no she's not. I had made plans to take her shopping with her aunt and that's what we are going to do."

"Well maybe you need to reschedule that day trip because like I said, I am her mother and she is coming with me."

What could Pier do? Monica was right but what burned Pier the most was the nerve that Monica had. She really felt like she could come and go as pleased. Pier wasn't going to stop her from going but she was going to make her understand once and for all that she was done dealing with her antics.

Monica got up and ran to Stacey's room. She scooped her up and tried to run but ran right into Pier who had begun to follow her. Pier inadvertently reached for Stacey because she was slipping out of Monica's arms. Stacey had no idea what was going on and began to cry. Monica tried to push past Pier thinking that Pier was trying to take Stacey from her and as she did they both dropped Stacey on the floor.

Stacey screamed at the top of her lungs. She tried to get up but couldn't. Her ankle looked twisted and began to swell rapidly.

"Look what you did you stupid bitch."

Pier ran and called 911 then Kyle. He met them at the hospital. Stacey ended up having a sprained ankle. The doctors put her in a soft cast because of her age and gave specific instructions that she stay completely off of her feet. He paid for Monica to take a cab to the house and get her car because she rode in the ambulance with Stacey and Pier drove herself back home where an infuriated Kyle met her.

Kyle didn't know if he should be angry at Monica for taking advantage of Stacey and basically forcing herself into the house or at Pier, who he had vehemently refused not to stoop Monica's level.

"Because you two couldn't control your tempers, Stacey is laying in the bed with a sprain. I thought I asked you not to engage in any type of altercation with her."

"You did but did you tell the bitch not to run up in this house? This is my house and you're acting as though I went looking for this to happen. You knew I had plans to spend the day with Stacey and Corrine and you're blaming me because you laid down with a whack job who you have absolutely no control over. If you should be mad at anybody it should be her."

"She's her mother. You should've let her take her and none of this would've happened."

"Are you saying that this is my fault?"

"I'm saying that you could've avoided it Pier."

"When are you going to stand up and be a man?"

"What did you say?"

"I said you act like a bitch when it comes to Monica!"

Kyle leaned into Pier. If another word had come out of her mouth, she believed he would've smacked her. She felt his anger and knew that she had crossed the line but she had to tell him how she felt. She was tired of being made out to be the bad guy. And now Stacey was hurt behind something that she did or didn't do. For that, she was sorry and it weighed heavy on her heart. She called Corrine and said that she needed to see her and that it was an emergency. Corrine rushed over.

"Pier, that trick is nuts, okay. How could you have known that she was going to pull a stunt like that? Damn girl she was just the nanny. What is she obsessed with, this child or Kyle?"

Pier didn't want to think about that. All she could think about was how angry she was. Monica had out done herself this time and Pier was at her wits end. She had to tell Corrine that she was Stacey's mother because maybe she would have a better understanding on what she was dealing with.

"WHAT?" That evil butt wart is her mother?"

"Yes." Pier put her head down onto the table.

"Pier, you are a better person than I am."

"Shush, lower your voice." Pier didn't want to wake Stacey or get Kyle started again. He had been in the bedroom with Stacey since they got home.

"What am I supposed to do? Leave because his daughter's mother hates my guts?"

"No you should've left his ass when he came up off of those lies he had told you. He came into this marriage lying so what makes you think that he's not still lying about something? I don't care what you say, it was wrong for him to lead you to believe that Stacey's mother was someone other than Monica. Hell I'd be pissed too if I were her but that's a normal person's re-action. She's a crazy chick and it's not going to stop here."

"Corrine, I am so lost. I don't know what to do and every time I go to Kyle about it he tells me to be the big-ger person. Don't feed into her craziness. I'm beginning to think that I'm the crazy one."

"And that's exactly what he wants you to think. Don't let him control and manipulate you. You better speak up and tell that brother how you feel and that you didn't sign up for this mess. He needs to get that chick under some kind of control or Pier, somebody is going to get hurt and it will be far worse than a sprained ankle."

Corrine was right. Pier had a feeling that things were going to get way worse before they got better as well.

Stacey had to stay home from school for several weeks. Kyle had to take off of work because Pier still had her everyday errands to do and somebody needed to be home to take care of Stacey. Monica had suggested that she come and stay with her, but Kyle decided otherwise. Enough trouble had been caused by Monica's bright ideas.

Pier had gone food shopping and to the cleaners. When she returned home there was an unfamiliar car parked in front of her house. She got out of her car and just as she did, the gentlemen got out of his. He walked towards her and introduced himself.

"I'm Mr. Best and I'm from the Division of Youth and Family Services."

All Pier heard was Division of Youth and Family Ser-vices. DYFS.

"I need to have a word with you if I may."

"What is this about?"

"There was a call into our office regarding a minor child Stacey Evans."

"And what was the call about?"

"Neglect. Miss, can we step inside please?"

Pier led the way into the house and immediately called out to Kyle. He came out from the back. The man introduced himself again and explained the nature of his visit. Pier and Kyle listened intently.

"We got an anonymous call that a child had fallen under the supervision of Pier Evans. Is that you?" He asked Pier.

"Yes that's me. Who made this call?"

"We are not at liberty to disclose that information and again it was an anonymous call."

"The hell you're not," Kyle interjected.

"It was Monica," Pier whispered.

"Why are you here man?"

"I am here to research this allegation and report whether the child is in a safe environment or not. Where is the child?"

"She's asleep in her bed. She has a sprained ankle." Kyle was furious.

"And are you the father?"

"Yeah."

"And are you the mother?

"No," Pier felt so awkward.

"Yes I see. Where is the mother?"

"She doesn't live here."

"I need to see the child please."

"No I don't think so. She's resting and I will not disturb her."

"For my records I need to see that the child is safe. If you refuse I will have to report this and there may be consequences."

Kyle knew from his experience that the man wasn't lying. He had no choice but to lead him to Stacey and show him that she was okay. The man stuck his head in the room, jotted notes on his note pad and went back to where they were sitting.

"I now have to present you with this waiver. Since this incident involved one other than the child's natural parents, Pier needs to sign this waiver that states that she will not use any type of force, or discipline the child under any circumstances. If the child requires discipline, it should be at the discretion of one of its biological parents."

"Force? I didn't use any force. Her mother grabbed her out of my arms and pushed me. That's how she fell. I didn't force anything."

"Miss I understand that but if you refuse to sign and she is hurt in the future, you risk losing her. If you so much as pluck her hair, pinch her ear or even spank her when warranted and we find out, she can be removed from the home until a full investigation is done."

"Sign it," Kyle said softly.

"What?" Pier was shocked.

"Sign it and I'll work it out later."

A distraught Pier signed the waiver then excused herself. She got her purse and keys and left the house. She needed some air. The walls were closing in on her and she felt like a rat running in a one-way maze that never ended.

The air outside was brisk. She stopped at the liquor store and bought a bottle of wine and a wine opener. Then she took a ride down to Belmar beach. She opened the bottle and drank. The tears came rolling down her face. Kyle had once again under minded her as his wife. And Monica had pulled yet another trick out from her bitch hat, one that unstabilized Pier and left her helpless. She couldn't have been that smart to know to pull

such a stunt. Working in the police department, she
must've heard or even read about such cases where
DYFS would get involved.

About an hour later she went home. Kyle was waiting
for her in the kitchen. She walked past him and went
straight to bed. He came in behind her.

"I'm going out for a while," Kyle said.

She didn't respond.

"Pier!"

"I heard you."

When he left she went and checked in on Stacey who
was asleep. She was given children's Tylenol with
codeine for the pain and that kept her asleep for hours
on end. Her tiny body lay so still. Pier looked at the light
pink cast that the doctor put on her. She leaned over
and gave her a kiss on her forehead. Her little arms
reached up and kissed Pier back on the nose. Pier took a
shower and got in the bed, finishing the last of the wine
that she bought and fell asleep.

"Open the door Monica. I've had it with you. You better open the door before I blow the lock off with my
gun. I don't care anymore about my job. You can call
them but you better open this door right now."

Monica was well aware of Kyle's temper. She'd seen it
many times when she pulled her mess in the past. On
several occasions he smacked her around for either running her mouth or trying to cause him grief at the job.
This time was big though. He knew that DYFS would
send a full report to his job and internal affairs would
include it in his file. He cocked his gun when she didn't
answer.

"I'm not going to warn you again."

She unlocked the door. He opened it and walked in
not closing it behind him. She was leaning up against

the sink. Kyle grabbed her by the neck, lifted her up and against a nearby wall.

"I've told you many times before not to push me. I don't appreciate the trouble you've caused me Monica. Do you realize what I'm going to have to deal with when I go back to work?" He squeezed tighter and she gasped for air.

"You've done it this time. I tried to give you a little say-so in Stacey's life and you've gone overboard. If you step one foot near my house without my knowing, I'm going to kill you. If you start one ounce of trouble with Pier, I will kill you and if you ever put Stacey's life in danger again, I will kill you. Do you under no uncertain terms understand what I just said to you?"

By then she was bright red. He had grabbed her neck so tight that if he held her a minute more, she would have fallen unconscious. She nodded once. He let her down and placed his gun on the table. She fell to the floor when he went to close the door. He sat in a nearby chair. Neither one of them said anything. Kyle needed time to get it together and Monica needed to catch her breath.

"I'm her mother. You treat me as an option, not with the respect a mother should have."

"Like I said, if you try anything else I'm going to kill you." He got up, grabbed his gun and left.

Monica stayed on the floor. Her neck hurt from his grip. She felt it and it was hot. Her pale complexion showed every flaw and she just knew that he'd left marks on her neck. In the past when they'd had arguments, he would still have sex with her. It was their distorted way of making up, even though they weren't together. All it meant was that the moment he got the feeling, she would be there to give him whatever he needed. Whether or not this time was different, she was unsure. All she knew was that he'd taken any special privileges that he may have given to her and threw them out the window. The one thing that remained true was that she was Stacey's natural and biological mother and she had rights to her if nothing else and she was going to invoke them.

Chapter Eighteen

Kyle took it upon himself to go down to the station and explain what had happened. Not to his surprise when he got there, there were notes in his mail box for him to see the director immediately when he returned to duty. He walked to the back where the director's office was located and knocked.

"Come in."

Kyle walked in. The director was on the telephone and motioned to Kyle that he would only be a minute. Kyle took a seat in one of the chairs that sat before his desk. When the director got off of the phone, he handed Kyle a folder. It was his personal file. When he opened it, the report from DYFS was there.

"I also got a call this morning from Monica. She explained what happened and well, you know the procedure."

And he did, all too well. He'd seen other cops have to hand in their weapons because one of their wives took their argument too far and reported them to the department. With domestic abuse being at an all time high, the department did not sweep under the carpet any complaint no matter how big or small. They took your weapon until a full investigation was done. In most cases the officer was mandated to take anger management classes and see a psychologist. They had to take and pass a series of tests and exercises. Once they completed their program the wife or girlfriend was notified that they received treatment and asked if they were okay with the officer having their weapon back. If they said no, then further investigation would ensue.

Kyle took his gun off and put it on the director's desk. He was also ordered to surrender any weapons that he had at the house. Two detectives would escort him home and do a search of the house for any weapons.

"Internal Affairs are on their way over to Monica's house to get a full report. You can go home and make sure you give up every weapon Kyle. I'm sorry but I need you back here first thing in the morning."

On the drive home, Kyle looked in his rear view mirror and saw the detectives following him. He shook his head in disbelief that he had allowed Monica to get him in such a volatile position. He was used to being in charge and now it seemed that depending on what she said, she could have his job. Then he thought about how he was going to explain this to Pier. He was sure that nothing that he said would make her believe that he did what he did for her and their marriage, so that they could live in peace instead of for his own selfish reasons.

He walked into the house and led the detectives to two rooms, which held his extra guns. They were locked in a gun locker. He asked that they be as quiet as possible because he didn't want to wake Pier up but that couldn't happen. While he surrendered his weapons, they still had to perform a search of the residence to guarantee that there weren't any other places that he hid weapons.

Kyle went into the bedroom and they followed him. The bottle of wine that Pier drank had put her in such a deep sleep that she didn't hear him call out to her. He came over and vigorously shook her, startling her out of her sleep.

"Get up Pier. These detectives need to search the bedroom for weapons. Disoriented, she grabbed her covers and tried to cover herself up. She was fully dressed but strange men were in her room and she didn't feel comfortable with that.

"What?"

"Just sit and be still. Let them search the bedroom and I will explain all of this to you later."

Pier sat back against the headboard. She immediately began to worry and feel anxiety. Kyle stood away as the detectives searched the bedroom and watched Pier watch them tear up the room. When they were finished, he followed them to the other rooms that needed to be searched and then in the basement, where they found another gun.

They gave Kyle a paper that he had to sign which swore that he had no other weapons in the house and that to the best of his knowledge, he surrendered any and all weapons that he had. When they were finished, he saw them out. He checked on Stacey and went back into the bedroom where he began to explain.

"I lost it. I went over there to talk to her about calling DYFS on you and she attacked me. I tried to get her off of me but all she kept on doing was trying to smack me and shit. Then she went for my gun and I had to stop her. I pulled it on her and told her to back off and that if she didn't I'd be forced to use it. Well you know she told a completely different story to my job."

"She called your job?"

"Yes and that's why they were here. They made me surrender my duty gun and any guns that I had here. There will be an investigation and baby I could lose my job."

Pier didn't think it was a good idea for an "I told you so" so she just kept quiet while he went on.

"She can have me fired. The very thing that I was most afraid of can happen to me. I can lose everything behind this woman and I'm scared." He needed Pier's sympathy because if she went off on one of her tangents and co-signed anything that Monica said by telling that he threatened her in the past too, together they could seal his fate.

Pier didn't completely understand the full magnitude of this investigation until she demanded to go with Kyle the following morning. Monica was in one room and was accompanied by counsel and Pier and Kyle were in another. Monica gave her account of what had happened and Kyle told the same story that he told Pier. Unfortunately, Monica's story prevailed and he was ordered on desk duty, also known as the rubber gun squad.

"Based on these findings, you are to complete a twelve step anger management course and schedule six months of therapy with a court-appointed psychologist. And you should know that this will go to the Prosecutor's Office for further review. If they feel that the requirements that we set forth are not enough, they are at liberty to mandate more or even harsher punishment. Also, Monica's lawyer is with her and he needs to hand you some paperwork. Do you think you need an escort to receive them?"

Kyle shook his head no. The lead Internal Affairs officer stepped out of the room and let a woman in. She introduced herself as Monica's lawyer and served him with child custody and child support papers.

"You've been served," was all she said. She turned around and walked out. Through the glass window, he could see Monica join her. She had her neck wrapped up in something that implied she was hurt. Pier jumped up to run after but was stopped by an officer.

"Ma'am, that wouldn't be a wise move."

She turned and screamed at the top of her lungs. Her insides were twisting and her head was heavy. She closed her eyes and saw spots in every color of the rainbow. They flashed in and out, then turned to black and white and then everything went completely black. She had passed out.

Pier was immediately transported to the hospital. Corrine spoke to the nurse and they had explained that she had hyperventilated and that's what caused her to pass out. If her vital signs were stable and she ate and kept food down, she could be released the next morning. Pier looked gray, tired and ashen from the recent events in her life. Kyle couldn't come to the hospital because he was home with Stacey, which was fine with Corrine. She didn't want him near her sister. She came and sat next to her. When she got the call from Kyle that Pier was admitted into the hospital, she called April and Renee. They were on their way.

She softly rubbed Pier's hand. They were sisters and best friends. If only Pier had listened to her and not married Kyle, she wouldn't be lying in that hospital. And if she had listened to her own gut and what it made her feel about Monica, she wouldn't be laying there either. As with anything and anybody, Corrine surmised, Pier had to learn the hard way.

It was late afternoon when Pier finally woke up to see April, Corrine and Renee by her side. Corrine hurried and called the nurse in so that she could check Pier's vitals.

"Don't worry girl, we're going to get you out of here and home where you belong. It won't be long," April assured Pier.

"Do we have to take her back to her house? Can't we take her to one of our houses?" Renee asked

"No," Pier managed to say. "I want to go home."

"There you go. She wants to go home."

The good news was that everything looked good. Her vitals were at good levels. All she had to do was eat something, keep it down, go to the bathroom and then she could be released to go home. The nurse also told them that she had some more good news.

"You're pregnant. According to our records you're about six weeks."

Pier looked in the opposite direction of everybody and began to cry. Corrine and April ran to her side, while Renee asked the nurse if she was sure. She was. Renee stood at the end of Pier's bed and rubbed her feet.

"Well looks like we got a baby shower to plan," she said in an effort to liven up the moment.

"Pier, this is a blessing. God has blessed you with an angel of your own to love. Don't let what's going on in your life take away from this moment. Everything will work out fine."

Nothing any of the girls said made Pier feel any better. As if her life wasn't in enough disarray, she was going to bring a baby into this mess she had as a marriage. She felt for sure God was punishing her for not listening to the signs he sent her before she even said I do to Kyle.

That evening she was discharged. April, Renee and Corrine took her home. They got her in the shower, made her some tea and put her in the bed. They got Stacey and sat her in the bed with Pier. Renee grabbed some blankets from Stacey's room and the closet and she, April and Corrine crashed on the floor below Pier and Stacey. During the night, Corrine got thirsty and went into the kitchen to get some water. She noticed Kyle sitting on the couch looking at a blank television. His look of defeat was a pleasure to Corrine's eyes because she felt with all the heartache that he caused her sister, he was getting everything that he deserved. Nonetheless, she went in and sat in a chair opposite him.

"We found out this afternoon that my sister is pregnant."

He slowly lifted his eyes to meet hers. He wasn't in the mood to listen to anything she had to say and he definitely wasn't thinking about having a baby. He was consumed with a problem way more important to him than an unborn child, losing his daughter and losing his job behind Monica. He looked away from Corrine.

"Did you hear me? She's having your baby you selfish, egotistical son of a bitch." She tossed her cold water in his face and went back to the bedroom. She locked the door to make sure he couldn't get in.

"What was that all about?" April asked.

"I told him that Pier was pregnant and he didn't even say a word. I hate his guts."

Kyle took a pillow off of the couch and wiped his face. Then he pulled out the phone book and looked up lawyers. He would need to secure one if he had a chance in hell in getting even shared physical custody of Stacey and keeping his job.

* * *

Stacey lay next to Pier awake and stared at Pier as she slept. Renee, April and Corrine were still asleep on the floor. Stacey put her face close to Pier's. With each exhale Pier took, Stacey felt her breath. She tapped her on the head. Pier woke up to tiny lips trying to hold in a laugh. Pier smiled and reached to tickle Stacey on her stomach. Her giggle woke up the others.

"Hey, some of us are trying to get some sleep you know."

"Aww hush. You wanted me awake so here I am. And I'm hungry. Who has the stove this morning?"

"We all do."

"May I have some eggs?" Stacey asked.

"Please," Pier said.

"Please."

Pier slowly got out of the bed. She felt drained. For sure she was emotionally drained, then she suddenly remembered what the nurse had told her. She was pregnant.

"What am I going to do?"

They knew what she was talking about.

"You're going to have this baby Pier. What else should you do? You conceived a baby with your husband. You act like you weren't entitled to do so, like you're not worthy. I wish you would stop allowing him to take your self-esteem away. You're not that weak."

"You just don't know what I've been going through these last couple of months. From the first day of my honeymoon, I've been dealing with his and Monica's mess. I didn't tell you guys because I didn't want to hear that you told me so. I tried to look at the bright side of things but every time I did, something happened and there was no longer a bright side. I've been arguing and fighting with Monica so much that she," Pier pointed to Stacey who listened but had no clue as to what they were really talking about, "got hurt. I felt like crap and it wasn't even my fault. The crazy woman called DYFS on us and now we're in the system. It's just been off the hook and I can't take it any more. I feel like I'm on the verge of a nervous breakdown."

Corrine got up and sat on the bed next to Pier. She wasn't going to let her sister fall to the wayside behind some man. She was going to help her sister get well so that she could have a healthy pregnancy and eventually help her leave Kyle.

"I told him that you were pregnant and he didn't blink an eye. He looked right through me as if I wasn't even there. Pier I'm telling you this man has no soul. He's out for self and that's it. Get better, have this baby and you are going to be the best mother any child could want."

"You told him? I didn't want to tell him just yet. I wasn't 100% sure that I was going to keep it. And from what you said, he could care less if I did or didn't. I can't talk about this anymore. Let's go and make a big breakfast."

They made eggs, bacon, pancakes, grits and cut up some fruit. Even Stacey had more than her usual request. They didn't talk about anything that had to do with what was going on. They talked about taking Stacey shopping when she could walk and maybe going away for the weekend some time soon. Even after they finished breakfast, they sat and talked as if they hadn't seen each other in years. They reminisced about their college days and high school sweethearts, wondering where they would be if they had made different choices in life. It was a happy conversation, and what everybody needed.

Pier explained to Stacey who Corrine, April and Renee were. Stacey was happy to find out that she had not one, not two but three auntie's who loved her and wanted to spend time with her. When they were finished, Pier and

Stacey sat while Renee and Corrine cleaned up the dishes. April went back to sleep.

Kyle found a lawyer that could see him on short no-tice and was located in Asbury Park off of Main Street. He had an 11:00 appointment that morning. While he was waiting, his phone rang. It was Monica. He ignored the telephone call when the receptionist told him that he could go into the office and meet with the lawyer

After he disclosed all of the facts, Kyle got some not so good news.

"It seems like you've been lucky up to this point. The fact that you have nothing in writing where your daugh-ter's mother relinquished her parental rights means you don't have the right to assume primary physical custody of the child. In fact, in most cases, that goes to the mother of the child unless she was found unfit. There is such a thing as joint physical custody, whereas you would have just as much say as she did with regards to where she goes to school and you would be included in parent-teacher conferences and things of the like. But depend-ing on how this investigation goes, you may lose cus-tody temporarily until you finish the required courses. And even after that, if they find that you were negli-gent or posed serious physical harm to Monica, you may only earn supervised visitation. Now there is the other issue of child support. I know you said that you have been giving her a certain amount every month as pay-ment for being or pretending to be the nanny, but we may be able to get that lowered. Now that she wants to play hardball, everything must be done by the books."

"Do whatever you can to keep me out of court. I want to settle this thing without appearing in front of a judge."

"I will have to do some heavy negotiating, you do realize that, and you may end up with less than what you have now with regards to your daughter."

"Look, I just found out that my wife is pregnant. I've already been stripped of my weapon and put on desk duty indefinitely. I'm not trying to face a judge who will only further humiliate me. I want this done as soon as possible and as quiet as possible.

"Okay. I understand."

Stacey was due to have her cast taken off the following week. Pier took her because since the incident with Monica, she hadn't called for Stacey or tried to see her. It was Pier's assumption that she was going to play the victim role out as much as she could and blame them for her not being able to see Stacey, or at least Kyle. But the child needed to be taken to the doctor nonetheless and since Kyle was nowhere to be found, Pier had to take her.

Her ankle was on its way to a full recovery. The doctor took the cast off with specific instructions for Stacey to refrain from running and any type of strenuous activity for the next few weeks.

When they arrived back home, Pier helped Stacey out of the car and into the house. On the door was a yellow USPS sticker that stated there was a letter waiting at the post office that required a signature, so back in the car they went.

"May I please see your driver's license?" The clerk asked Pier.

She handed it over to him. Pier signed for the letter and left. When she got in the car, she opened it even though it was addressed to Kyle. It was from his lawyer and stated that he had been in touch with Monica's lawyer and they were ready to talk negotiations. There was a specific time and date stated and he was to call and confirm that he would be there. She was excited that they may be able to handle the matter quickly, but then she was also still pissed that Monica had put them in that situation.

When Kyle got home that evening, Pier told him about the letter.

"Why did you sign for it? It was addressed to me not you."

"I thought I was doing you a favor by going and getting it for you. Figured it would be one less thing that you would have to worry about but I guess I was wrong. By the way, I'm pregnant." She tossed the letter to him.

He didn't respond. He opened the letter, read it and immediately called his lawyer's office to confirm the appointment that was set for that Friday at 9:00 in the morning. Pier had gone into the living room and put in a movie. Kyle came and sat next to her.

"I thought you were being careful."

"What are you talking about now Kyle?"

"I thought I told you that I didn't want any more children. Wait, what I mean is this is not the right time to bring a child into our marriage."

"You can't truly think that I planned to get pregnant. Give me a break Kyle. I was just as surprised to find out as you were. But you should be getting the picture that you can't always get what you want, not anymore it seems."

Pier tried to let him know that his controlling and self-centered ways were about to be the death of him. He walked around like the world owed him something or that he deserved more respect than the next person.

"If I lose my job, how do you think we are going to support this child? How will we pay the bills?"

"I'll get a job."

"Doing what?"

"What do you mean doing what? Contrary to what you've been used to I have a college degree. I can get a job doing whatever I want to do. The baby and I will be okay."

"The baby and you? What about me?"

"What about you Kyle? You created this monster. You wanted to have your cake and eat it to."

"You're right. I did and still do. I'm leaving for a while."

"Bye!"

When Kyle got in the car, he made a bold decision and called Monica. She was waiting for him to call back and knew that it was only a matter of time. She explained to him the reason for her call.

"Well, I think that we could work this out amongst the lawyers but perhaps we, you and I, can come to some sort of prearranged agreement."

"Okay. And what's in it for me?"

"I'll admit that I grabbed Stacey from Pier and caused her to fall. I'll do what I can to get the charges dropped and say that I was just angry that you fired me."

"First, you can't drop the charges Monica. It went to the prosecutor's office and it's out of anybody's control so thanks but no thanks."

"Maybe I can write a letter. Think that will work?"

"In exchange for what Monica? I've had it with your bullshit. Maybe it's good that all of this went down because now I don't have to kiss your ass anymore."

"Don't be so sure about that. Why don't I come over and talk with you and Pier? I'm sure that we can work something out."

"First of all I'm not home. Second, you are the last

person that Pier is interested in seeing and third, she's pregnant so please do us all a favor and stay away from her."

"How is Stacey?"

"You haven't called to speak to her or picked her up since all of this mess went down."

"Well I'd like to see her."

"Not tonight."

Kyle's response made Monica angry. Who did he think he was telling her that she couldn't see her own daughter? She too was tired of him controlling her. He wanted her at the house just as much as she wanted to be there. He had sex with her every night and even came home in the middle of the night when he worked midnights and fucked her. Kyle called all the shots because he knew how Monica felt for him and he knew that she wanted to be there with Stacey. When Pier came into the picture he changed up on her even more. And even more so now that she was pregnant and was going to have his baby.

"Yes tonight."

"Monica, I'm not in the mood,"

CLICK

"Hello! Hello! Fucking Bitch!"

Monica got dressed and went over to the house. Pier heard her pull up and tried to call Kyle. It went right to his voice mail. She went to the door and opened it.

"Monica, Kyle isn't here."

"Oh hi Pier, I'm not here to see Kyle. I was wondering if Stacey was up and if I could see her."

"You know I think that with everything that's going on, it would be wise to wait until Kyle was home."

"Are you denying me the right to see my child?"

"Don't you think you should've arranged this before hand rather than just showing up at my house?"

"Probably, but that's irrelevant. I'm here now and want to see my daughter."

Pier went to close the door in Monica's face. Monica kicked the door at the same time and pushed her way in. Pier grabbed her by the shirt and they fell onto the floor. Monica pulled at Pier's head while Pier tried to push her off of her. She was too big and Pier wasn't able to do so. Monica moved her body up so that Pier was between her legs and began to punch her in the face and head. Every time Pier went to swing at her, her heavy arms blocked her and Monica was able to get Pier every time either in the face, chest or head. Pier got tired of trying to get a grip of Monica and figured if she kicked her legs and wiggled her body hard enough, she could get from under her and gain control of the situation. With a few intense movements she was able to move from under Monica at which point she used all of her might to push her. As Monica fell over, she hit her head on a nearby table and fell unconscious.

A breathless Pier panted as she looked over at Monica's lifeless body. Just as she went to see if she was still breathing, Kyle busted through the door. He looked at the scene before him and was speechless.

"She," Pier tried to speak.

Kyle walked a circle around Monica's large body then looked over at Pier. He noted that the house was disheveled.

"She came in here and attacked me."

"Okay." He stood and thought. As foul as it seemed, it was perfect. Monica had come there and attacked Pier. Pier defended herself and as a result, Monica fell and hit her head on the table. Now all he needed to do was determine if she was really dead or still alive. He knelt down and felt for a pulse. He didn't find one.

"We have to call 911." Pier said in an exasperated voice.

"Where is Stacey?"

"In her room. Give me the phone so I can call 911." Kyle ignored her. He knocked down a few more things in the living room so that there appeared to be more of a struggle than there was. He looked at Pier. He realized that this was his chance to get Monica out of his life for good, so he went into the kitchen and grabbed a dish towel. He came back into the living room, grabbed a medium sized statue that sat on the end table and hit Pier in the head just enough to leave a mark that would further justify what she did to Monica.

"Kyle, why?" Pier moaned.

He reached down again and felt for a pulse and again he didn't find one. To make sure she was a done deal he lifted her up with great effort and dropped her head against the table again. Monica was gone.

"Now we can call 911."

Chapter Nineteen

It seemed like the ambulance took forever to get there. Pier had since fallen into a light sleep. Kyle had gotten her some ice for her head and lay her on the couch. The paramedics were removing Monica's body when Kyle was called out of the house by a homicide detective. He explained to him what he thought happened and said that this was the story that he got from Pier. Kyle knew the drill and wasn't surprised when the officer told him that he would need to get a statement from Pier.

"In the morning man, right now I want to get her to the hospital. She's pregnant with our child and I want to make sure she's going to be okay. So let me get her into the ambulance and to the hospital and I promise you that you can speak with her in the morning."

Kyle was working off of pure adrenaline. His heart raced a mile a minute. He couldn't go with Pier to the hospital because he had no one to watch Stacey. And besides, he wanted to stay at the house and help the detectives, more or less watch them. They took pictures of Monica's body and the surrounding area.

"Boy, she was really pissed with you huh Captain"? one cop said.

"Well yeah, you know we all have at least one nut case from our past."

It took three paramedics to lift Monica without dropping her. Blood dripped from her head and onto the furniture. She slipped out of one of their hands and Kyle caught her. As they got a better handle of her body, Kyle looked at his hands. He had her blood on them.

After all the commotion had died down, Kyle thought he'd better call Corrine and tell her what happened to Pier.

"Where is she?"

"She's at Monmouth Medical. I wasn't able to go because there is no one to watch Stacey."

"Okay. I'll go."

He sat on the edge of his bed and went over everything he did over and over again in his mind. He recited everything that he saw from the moment he stepped into the house.

I came into the house and saw Pier lying over there, he thought. In his mind he pointed to the couch, Monica, and to a spot on the floor. *I asked Pier what had happened but she was barely conscious and couldn't tell me. I reached down and felt for a pulse on Monica and when I couldn't find one, I called 911.*

"Perfect!" He whispered. Kyle went into Stacey's room and checked in on her. It's a wonder that she wasn't awakened with all of the commotion. He bent down and softly called her.

"It's Daddy baby, wake up."

She turned over and smiled at him.

"How are you sweetheart? Is your ankle all better?"

She nodded yes.

"Come let me make you something to snack on." He lifted her up and carried her into the kitchen. He sat her down, took out some cheese and crackers and placed them in front of her. Then he poured himself a glass of wine and sat next to her.

As he watched her eat, he thought about how everything had played out. His luck hadn't run out like Pier and Monica thought it had. Monica's untimely death was on time for him and his situation. Since Monica was no longer around to confirm any alleged charges against him, he was confident that when he met with his lawyer on Friday he would tell him that his chances of getting his case thrown out were great. Stacey was going to miss her mother but his thoughts were that she was young enough to bounce back. Children were resilient. With a few therapy sessions and constant praising of how wonderful her mother was, Stacey would grow up thinking that her mother had an awful accident and was now in heaven with the angels.

Pier on the other hand wouldn't have such luck. If Kyle had left Monica the way she was, not only would she have possibly survived but Pier may only have been charged with manslaughter. Now that she was dead, at the very least she would be charged with negligent homicide and was sure to get some jail time. He hated to do it but he had no choice.

When Pier woke up the following morning, she was disoriented. Her head was hurting her badly. She reached and touched her forehead and felt that it was wrapped up. She opened her eyes and saw a blurried vision of Corrine who sat by her side. She looked past her and saw a doctor reading a chart.

"Where am I?"

"Pier, you're in the hospital. There was a terrible accident."

"What? What happened?"

"Pier, Monica is dead. She came to the house last night and attacked you. Unfortunately in protecting yourself, she fell and hit her head on the end table. I'm sorry."

Pier shook her head. "No, that's not what happened."

She thought she remembered seeing Kyle come into the house and bend down over Monica. Or did she see him check her pulse? Or did she see him drop her onto the table? She wasn't too out of it to remember telling him to call 911 and him not doing so. She wasn't too out of it to remember that she saw him mess up the house even more than it was. But who would believe her or better yet, what was going to happen to her now that Monica was dead?

"There's Pier," Kyle said as he and Stacey walked into Pier's room. Pier turned away because she didn't want to look at Kyle.

"Hey pudding," Corrine reached for Stacey. "Want to see Pier?"

Kyle walked over to the doctor and inquired about Pier's condition.

"And what about the baby?"

"I'm sorry, she miscarried," the doctor said.

Corrine looked over at Kyle. He felt her looking at him and began to act if he were crying. He covered his face and shook a little to add a little spice to his act. He fell against the wall and rubbed his eyes until they watered. Then he sniffed a bit, wiped his face with his forearm and went over to Pier's bedside.

"Honey, I have some bad news. You lost the baby."

Corrine, who was gently bouncing Stacey on her hip

froze. Pier turned to Kyle then she looked over at her sister and Stacey and began to cry.

"Oh Pier, it will be okay," Corrine tried to tell her.

"Why is Pier crying?" Stacey wanted to know. Pier held her arms out and Corrine lowered Stacey to her face. She gave her a kiss and turned over in her bed.

The doctor thought it was a good time for Pier to get some rest. Corrine asked Kyle if she could speak to him in the hallway.

"I don't know. I came home and found them both on the floor. Pier was gasping for air and Monica was just laying there. I called 911 when I couldn't get a pulse. This is terrible. I mean we had our differences but now Stacey lost her mother and Pier lost our baby. I don't know why this is happening to us."

"What's going to happen with Pier? She was defending herself. Will they understand that or is she going to jail?"

"It's too soon to tell."

Just as Kyle said that, two detectives walked up and into Pier's room. She turned over when she heard them come in.

"Pier Evans?"

"Yes."

"You are under arrest for murder. You have the right to remain silent."

Kyle and Corrine watched as Pier was read her Miranda rights. They cuffed her to the bed and placed her under arrest. Anything and everything that was before Pier began to fade away. She was lying in a hospital bed with a busted head that Kyle gave her and under arrest for the death of Monica, who came to her home and attacked her. Her life as she knew it prior to Kyle didn't exist anymore. Her life with Kyle landed her in the situation that she was in now, and ultimately would land her behind bars. For the rest of her stay in the hospital, which consisted of a week, Pier had to be sedated because she couldn't stop crying.

When Pier felt well enough, she was transported to the county jail for arraignment. Corrine and Kyle were there when her bail was set at $500,000 which needed to be paid in cash or bond. Corrine, April, Renee and Kyle were in court with her.

"Don't look at me Corrine, I don't have that type of money," Kyle left the courtroom.

Since Kyle claimed he didn't have the money to post bail for her and since between Corrine, April and Renee they were only able to scrape up $20,000, Pier remained in jail.

"The very least you can do is hire a lawyer Kyle. Your wife is sitting in jail." Corrine argued.

"I'm facing charges myself. I need my money to give to my own lawyer. Why don't you use the money that you, April and Renee have and get her a lawyer?"

"You're a useless asshole. I told her from the door that you were a no good stinking bastard. You use and manipulate people. And to think she went ahead and married your sorry ass anyway. Yes, we will use our money. And for the record fuck you Kyle."

Corrine's words didn't faze Kyle. In fact they fell on deaf ears because not only did the prosecutor's office send his case back to his department to handle, when he went and saw his lawyer, he was advised that he didn't have to attend any classes or seek any professional help. It was suggested, however, that he voluntarily took parenting classes and joined a group that catered to people who lost a spouse. He was also advised to get Stacey into therapy. When he agreed, he was awarded full custody of her.

Kyle was relieved but there was one person who could still do him some harm, Pier. He had to take steps that would make sure that she was put away long enough for him to divorce her and cut all ties completely.

Chapter Twenty

When she was being processed into the system, she had to strip down and be humiliated as every orifice of her body was searched. The group shower that she had to take further demeaned her because she had to take it together with the other new inmates, a few of which were on their third and fourth visit.

Pier looked around her cell. The gray walls that formed the 5 x 7 room were cracked and decorated with writings from previous inmates. The bed had a 2-inch thick mattress and was held up by wire that couldn't be any thicker than that of which a hanger was made of. It's rickety build didn't allow much movement without making annoying squeaky sounds. There was a urinal in her cell and she imagined it was white at one point but its current state was that of a brownish yellow. The strong stench of urine would fill her lungs if she breathed in too deeply and the whaling of the other inmates forced her into the corner of her bed where she balled herself up and hid her head by pulling her shirt up at the neck and pulling it over. It was cold and damp. Guards walked back and forth especially in front of the new inmate's cells because they were prone to committing suicide within the first couple of days of being detained.

With her eyes closed she went back to the day she met Kyle. There were clues everywhere and she ignored them. She thought about how he would do things that told her he was controlling but she still didn't back off. Kyle had danger written all over him that warned her of what she would be put through for loving him. She felt stupid. She felt like she should've listened to her sister and girlfriends. They saw something in him that she didn't. Instead of listening to them, she made excuses for his behavior and even defended him on several occasions.

Then there was Stacey, the innocent. She had no clue as to what happened and not only lost her mother but lost Pier. In retrospect, Kyle demonstrated extreme control over Stacey's life. He told Monica when she could take her, where she could take her and controlled the finances in which Monica needed to do anything with her. Not once did she see him give Monica her pay check. He must've deposited it into her account when he wanted to.

It was a week before Pier's lawyer showed up to speak with her. As she sat across from the woman, Pier was very overwhelmed with anxiety. She had no idea what to say to this lady. The woman sat and thumbed through papers for about fifteen minutes before she finally said something.

"I see that the deceased reported that your husband attacked her recently. It also says that you and her would argue at the sight of each other. In addition, it says that you initiated most of the arguments when she tried to see her daughter. Is that true?"

"No, that's not true. I did nothing but try to make the

relationship work. I didn't know that she was Stacey's mother until I was on my honeymoon with my husband. But yes, by then we had had a few arguments under our belts. I never wished this woman any harm though."

"So you never told Kyle that if you knew someone who could handle her, her ass would be handled that night?"

"No, he said that. She caused him more grief than I did. When we would have our arguments, both Monica and I would complain to him about each other."

"Okay. And you didn't go into her room one night and tell her that she had her place. You were with Kyle, she needed to get over it and that you weren't going to let her ruin what you and Kyle were trying to build together?"

"No, I'm telling you, Kyle said those things."

"Well, it makes it seem that you were jealous that she had Kyle's daughter and that he was still having sex with her forcing her to remain in your life. Also, it states that you would interfere with her visitation with their daughter."

"Where are you getting this information from? I didn't do anything to this woman. When we first met she was the one who gave me the hard time. Kyle said that she had been with him since Stacey was young. I had no idea that they had a relationship and had Stacey. Did you say that they were still sleeping together?"

"Yes. According to Kyle, he said that he told you before you and he got married that he was still involved with her. If you knew this and didn't agree with it, why did you stay if for no other reason but to get to her?"

"I'm telling you that that was not the case. And Kyle wasn't sleeping with her. They slept together in the past and that was it. He wasn't with her anymore."

Her lawyer pulled out a statement that Kyle made

with regards to her relationship with Monica. It stated that Kyle had advised Pier that he and Monica had been together and still got together on occasion. He also swore to the fact that when he told her, she initially had a problem with it but loved him and accepted it.

"That's bullshit, he's lying."

"Well that may be the case but he's not the one on trial for lying. You are on trial for murder and all of this that I just discussed with you will be admitted and spoken about at your trial. He has already painted an ugly picture of you as an angry wife who wouldn't accept his daughter and the relationship that he had with his daughter's mother. As optimistic as I want to be, it doesn't look good for us but as with any case, I will do my best to get you out of here."

"How is Stacey?"

"I don't know. I haven't seen or spoken to the child yet. But that is something that I plan to do. The relationship between you and her is crucial from the stand point of how comfortable she was with you, how you treated her and things of the like. She may be too young in the court's eyes. Maybe they will allow a court appointed therapist to speak with her. We'll see. Have you heard from your husband?"

"No."

"He hasn't come to see you?"

"Not since I was in the hospital. My sister is coming right after you though."

"That's good. Try and think positive."

As soon as her lawyer left, Corrine came in. Pier was glad to see her and tried to smile as much as she could but inside, her spirit was detached from her mind. Her soul was floating in limbo. The emotions that she had been feeling were new to her. She felt isolated, betrayed and unloved by the one man who she felt she went against everything for. She was alone once again.

"April and Renee wanted to come but they said that you could only have two visitors a day for now. How are you holding up? Do you need anything?"

"I'm doing as best as I can. Corrine, how did this happen? Why me?"

"Pier, I don't know how it happened. Life throws us some crazy curve balls sometimes. I'm sorry that you are going through this sis, I really am but we're here for you. We'll be by your side the entire way. Everything will work out."

It was difficult for Corrine to say those words to her sister because in her heart she herself didn't believe them. The charges that Pier faced would be backed up by the events that had taken place over the past months. More than likely things would not go in her favor when it came time to decide whether or not she was guilty.

"Can you see Stacey? Have you tried to contact Kyle and see if you could spend some time with her? Who is watching her after school now?"

"I haven't tried because to he honest with you, our last words weren't pleasant to each other. He didn't give any money towards your lawyer's fees. He said that he had his own problems. I cursed him out and left it at that."

"He won't let you see her then. He hasn't even been up here to see me. Do you know what it is like in here? I don't belong here. Corrine, I didn't kill Monica. She came there to see Stacey and tried to bust in the door. When I wouldn't let her in, she attacked me. We fell to the floor as we fought and she ended up on top of me. I kept trying to buck her off of me and when I finally did, she fell over and hit her head on the end table. Kyle had come home and saw me laying halfway on the couch and Monica was lying on the floor. She was still breathing because I heard her moaning. He stood there and looked at us. I told him to call 911 and he just continued to stand there. Then he lifted her up and hit her head on the coffee table again. That's what killed her."

"Did you tell your lawyer this? What did she say?"

"She knows but she said that with the history between Monica and I it shows that I had motive. I was a jealous wife who was angry at the relationship that she and Kyle had."

"He lied to you the whole time Pier. He made it seem like this woman was his nanny and she turned out to be the child's mother! Kyle fed you a bunch of lies from the door. He's, in part, responsible for Monica's death. And I'm going to talk to your lawyer about Kyle's statement. Again, he's lied about so much, I'm sure you're right when you say that he lied about what happened."

"But the jury won't see it that way Corrine."

"I know Pier, but we have to at least get someone to check into his account of what happened."

"I hate him. I hate him so much. I never thought that I could feel this way about someone. I did nothing but love him and his daughter. I didn't listen to those who told me that there was something about him that just wasn't right. He played me from day one."

"This is not the time to do this to yourself Pier. Stay strong and focused and tell the truth. My time is up. I will try to reach out to Kyle and see if I can see Stacey. Maybe take her out for a while. I will contact your lawyer as well."

"Yes, she would like that."

Corrine couldn't get out of that place fast enough before the tears flowed down her face. Pier looked like she had lost more weight, her hair was brash, her skin was pale and her spirit was invisible. She called April and Renee.

"I didn't know what to say to her. She looks so bad. I tried to be positive but she's going to stay in jail for a long time if the jury is convinced that she murdered Monica."

"Corrine, did Kyle tell them how Monica was? Did he mention that she caused a lot of the issues that they had, and that she would come there uninvited?"

"Renee, I don't know, but I want to, trust me. And the only people who know this is her and Kyle. I'm going to go over there and see if I can get Stacey for a while. Maybe, although I doubt it because I cursed his butt out for not helping us pay for Pier's lawyer, he'll open up a little and I can get some information that could help Pier."

"Want us to come?"

"No because then he may feel like we're ganging up on him. I'll go by myself."

Chapter Twenty-One

Linda sat across from Kyle in the kitchen. Monica wasn't just her assistant, they were friends. She had warned Monica on several occasions that the relationship that she had with Kyle wasn't a good one and that it was certain to blow up in her face sooner or later. But never did she think it would end up in her death.

"Kyle, you controlled this whole mess. What did you expect her to do? You've only been sleeping with her for God knows how long. You made her feel as if she as something special to you. She understood that you didn't want to marry her, but by you moving her into your place, giving her money, allowing her to do whatever she wanted in the house, made her think that she was more to you than what she was. Regardless if you've told her that you didn't want to be with her on a serious level, when Pier came into the picture and moved in, then got married, that was a smack in the face for Monica."

"That was my choice. Monica knew the deal from the door. She was a piece of ass that I liked having around. She did it to herself because she could've walked away any time. Not once did I tell her that if she stuck around things would change. She knew what I was about when we hooked up. She acted like she was thankful for just being in my presence. She wasn't going to control what I had going on. No, the others didn't move in but I fucked them in the next room just like I did Pier and I fucked her in her room when the others were doing whatever. She knew the game when she started to play."

"That's all well and fine but in her mind, you were her man. By you letting her live here, basically acting as your wife because she did everything for you, you allowed her to think that she was permanent. That no other woman would ever be able to come between you two."

"Did I tell her that? No! She was messed up in the head in my opinion, any time you put yourself in a position to be at someone's disposal 24 hours a day. What man wouldn't want a chick that was submissive to him 100% and would do anything for him? She lost focus. She forgot her purpose and that's why things turned out the way they did."

"And you can live with yourself knowing that you messed with her mind like that?"

"Yup. I don't have time to think about what happened and develop regrets because I don't regret being me. And Pier, I love her, I do but she did what she did and now she has to pay for it. My main focus is Stacey. I'm all she has right now."

"Who will care for her when you go to work?"

"I guess she will have to attend after school care or I'll hire another nanny."

Linda just looked at Kyle. They had been cool for years and she just couldn't stand the sight of him. He was so arrogant in how he spoke about Monica. He never cared about anybody but himself. Everything he did was for him and if somebody didn't serve a purpose in his life, he had no use for them.

"Have you gone to see Pier?"

"No. I'm not taking Stacey to a jail."

"Who said anything about Stacey? Why haven't you gone to see your wife in jail? You claim to love her, why haven't you gone to see if she was okay and how they were treating her? You're an officer and I'm sure you know someone in there that could keep an eye out for her. Or are you not concerned with her well-being? Let me ask you something, what was Pier's purpose?"

Corrine pulled up in front of the house. She saw that there was another car there and almost didn't go up to the door. But for Pier's sake, she needed get some answers.

Kyle was saved by the ring of the doorbell but was shocked to see Corrine standing at the door. He paused, then let her in. He introduced her to Linda and invited her in to have a seat.

"Corrine, how are you?"

"Fine. Listen I have some questions. I know that Pier and Monica had some arguments before this, but did you tell the officers how Monica would start trouble, come over here and get Stacey to let her in the house?"

"I explained to them that they didn't get along and that there was this constant battle over me, but I didn't give them any specific incidents, no."

"Why not? Wouldn't you think that it would help Pier's case if they knew that Monica was crazy? Pier never went to her place and started trouble. She was here, married to you and making a home for herself. I don't understand why you're not more supportive of her. If you didn't love her, why did you marry her? And your account of what happened doesn't match what my sister says. You can best believe that I'm going to point this out to her lawyer."

"Wait, what?" Linda asked.

"I do love her and like I said I told them everything I knew. My hands are tied. I'm not working this case, they are, and they are going to look at simple facts . . . Monica came here, yes, they argued and Monica ended up dead. That's it. I'm sorry that she has to go through this."

"She? That *she* is still your wife. And that's right, Pier said that Kyle came in after Monica had fallen and hit her head. She was still alive because Pier heard her moaning. According to Pier, Kyle came in and finished her off by picking her head up and hitting it on the table again."

Linda listened as Corrine went back and forth. Her loyalties were being challenged at that very moment. Should she go to the police and tell them the entire story about Monica? How she got involved with Kyle, the stipulations in which she was able to live in the same house as him with their daughter or should she let the police handle the investigation? Pier was going to do time no matter what, but how long she would be locked up could depend on something that Linda said. And now that Kyle may have given the deadly blow, Linda knew that she had to at least get him questioned further.

"I have to go."

"Linda, I'd like to finish this conversation," Kyle said.

"Sure. It was nice meeting you Corrine. I hope everything works out for your sister."

"Thank you." Corrine and Linda's eyes met for a split second. Kyle picked up on it but didn't say anything. When Linda left, he was a little more verbal.

"Why are you here? If it's to aggravate me about Pier and her situation, please save it."

"I'm not here to aggravate you Kyle. I just want to know why you have abandoned her. She was a good wife to you and a wonderful stepmother to Stacey. She never did anything to hurt you and stood by anything you said and this is how you repay her? She's sitting in a cell Kyle, in jail behind some mess that I think you had more to do with than you are saying."

"What? Are you accusing me of something?"

"I'm not accusing you of anything. I'm telling you that you had your hand in this shit from the door and it will only be a matter of time before what you did in the dark comes to light."

"You didn't like me from the beginning. You and your friends had it out for me ever since Pier and I hooked up. What, did one of you want me for yourself? We could've made that happen, man, it could've always been that type of party."

"You are crazy and in need of some serious help."

"Get out Corrine. You and I have no reason to talk."

Corrine stormed out of the house feeling like it was useless to even try and talk to Kyle. He was so stuck on himself that he couldn't see what he did to Pier, or Monica for that matter. Just as Corrine was about to pull off, Linda approached her.

"Can we talk?"

They rode to a nearby diner. Both ordered a cup of coffee. Linda had decided that to have all of this information about the relationship between Kyle and Monica and not say anything would be wrong. It wouldn't bring Monica back, but maybe if the authorities knew the entire story Pier may have a chance in getting a lighter sentence. Morally, she had to do it. As an officer of the courts, she had to make sure that everything was disclosed and that Pier had a fair trial. And she too would get Kyle's statement of what happened checked into.

"First I want to say that Monica was a very good friend of mine. I'm sorry for where your sister is at, but Monica was a victim here too."

"Okay," Corrine said.

"She and Kyle had a relationship of his convenience. When he worked late nights, she was available and he took advantage of that. She wasn't the most attractive person but that didn't matter for what Kyle wanted her for."

"Which was?"

"Sex with no strings attached."

"Until she got pregnant and then what?"

"They argued because she wanted more of a commitment from him, but he was married at the time. She leaked out that they were having an affair and his wife found out."

"What did his wife do? Did Kyle and Monica stop seeing each other?"

"No. In fact it was quite the opposite. He basically bribed them both. His wife wanted out, there was no question about that and to keep her quiet, he bought her out of the house *and* paid her mortgage when she bought another one. That's when he made a deal with Monica to allow her to move in and be a 'nanny' to Stacey."

"How did they keep this quiet all of this time? I mean didn't anybody question where this child came from? Monica was pregnant and showing obviously right? And no one at work questioned who the father was?"

"They may have and if they did, she knew not to say anything. Kyle's persona at work was his biggest concern. He needed people to think nothing but the best of him and if she slighted his reputation, she would've had hell to pay."

"How so, did he threaten her?"

"Yes. I've seen him smack her around a few times when she got slick with her mouth. Maybe she wanted to spend more time with him or maybe it was one of the days where she got fed up and told him. He was in full control of her. He paid her, maintained the rent on her own place."

"She didn't see the possible ramifications of giving someone that much control over her life? I mean as a woman, didn't she want more for herself, and Stacey?"

"She wanted to be where ever he was. She was in love with Kyle. He knew this and took advantage of it."

"Had she said anything to you about my sister being in his life?"

"She didn't like it of course and when he got married to her, well, she basically lost it. See, he never stopped having sex with her. The day of the party where we first met Pier, he had sex with her that night when your sister was in the shower. She told me this directly. He had sex with her the following morning too. There was no end to his control over her mind and she did whatever he wanted to make him happy. Again, she was so in love with him that she was willing to deal with any other woman in his life, but when he put her out, that's when things really started to get crazy."

"Would you be willing to tell this to Pier's lawyer?"

"Yes, this is why I came to you."

Chapter Twenty-Two

Corrine went to see Pier and told her everything that Linda has spoken to her about. She was devastated when she found out that Kyle was still having sex with Monica when they met.

"I can't believe this."

"I know it sucks but girl he was playing the both of you. He never ended whatever he had with Monica and that's why she was tripping when you came into the picture. Unfortunately, there is no legal punishment for what he did but if the jury knows how he did the both of you, maybe they will understand her frustration with you and why she was the way she was."

"How will that help me Corrine? I'm the one who is charged with her death, not Kyle or anybody else. Who else are they going to blame, her?"

"No, but he is so cold and callous about her death, Pier, that has to throw red flags up for someone."

"Maybe, maybe not. He had full control of this love triangle for lack of better words. If nothing else, it will let people know the type of person *he* is. His fellow police officers will know that behind that shiny badge and all of those awards, that they have a genuine asshole. He will lose any credibility he had. They won't respect him and Pier, the truth will be out there."

Pier got up. All of this was too much for her.

"Who told you all of this?"

"Linda. She said she met you at the party that April, Renee and I left. She was his lawyer."

"I take it she's not anymore."

"Monica was her friend too, Pier. What Kyle did and how he treated you was wrong. She wants to try and help you because both of you were the victims of his manipulation."

"Tell her thanks." She turned and motioned for the guard to come and get her. Corrine watched as her sister was led out of the visitor's room. She didn't turn back to say anything.

Linda and Corrine met up at Pier's lawyer's office and told her the entire story. And while she was receptive to the information and it did shed some light onto why Monica was so crazy about Kyle, it didn't negate the fact that she was dead and it appeared that Pier killed her.

"There must be something that you can use. What about the fact that Kyle showed no emotions about Monica's death?"

"What about it?" The lawyer asked. "Who said he had to be emotional about it? These two women were caught up in the middle of a love triangle. No, Pier didn't know that her husband was still having sex with Monica, but Monica's knowing that he had gone and gotten married had no bearing on what I'm dealing with here. She is facing charges on murder, not being naïve or making a bad choice."

"So nothing that we've told you will help her?"

"I want to go in the court room and give what I per-
ceive are the facts. I will have Kyle go over what he
walked in on and see if there are any holes in his account of things. Can I make the jury believe that Monica
was in a crazed mindset and went over there to cause
Pier some physical harm? Possibly. But to go in there and
give all these examples of his infidelity will do nothing
but make it seem like we're fishing for a reason as to
why this woman is dead other than the obvious. The
fact that she was in her home when she was defending
herself may go in her favor. Monica was an uninvited
guest, but other than that, unless we can get enough
money to post bail, Pier will remain in jail."

"I guess we'll just have to see where this goes then,
huh?"

"Yes."

The days leading up to Pier's trial were long. She tried
not to think too hard about what had taken place before she got to where she was. There was no point because she couldn't change anything about the decisions
that she made. Her days consisted of getting up, forcing
herself to eat the food that they served, reading and
writing in a journal. She had no interest in making any
friends there. All she wanted to do was keep to herself.

Corrine and Linda took it upon themselves and went
to Kyle's superiors and told them about the things that
Kyle had been doing. They were told that he was having
an affair with a co-worker and told them that it was Monica. They had their suspicions but when they inquired,
Kyle blew them off and Monica denied it completely.
There was nothing that they could do with this information, but as they had hoped, the news spread like wild-
fire. Unfortunately, no one treated Kyle any different.

His co-workers still treated him with respect because

to them, it was all hearsay. He was still captain, still held many commendations, still was the boss, still was good looking, still had control of anything that he wanted and could really care less even if people did start to treat hin differently. At the end of the day, his officers still reported to him and that was all he was concerned with. As long as he wasn't stripped of his badge or rank, he was still Captain Kyle Evans. He was, however, curious about how his business got back to his superiors. He paid Pier a visit.

"How are you?"
She didn't answer.
"Are they treating you good?"
Still no response.
"Okay, I'll get to the point. I know you were the one who told everybody about what had been going on. Yes, you stirred the pot a little, but Pier it didn't shake me. Do you really think that they are concerned about two women who were in love with me? You and Monica just didn't get it and now that everybody knows, not only my business, but yours too, they think that Monica was crazy and you were stupid. Stupid to not only stay with me, but to marry me knowing that I was still sexually involved with my daughter's mother and that I was just a man doing what men do."

"Kyle, I loved you. Everything you did and said was done and said in vain. The sad thing Kyle, is that Stacey has no one other than you to look up to as a role model. Poor child, her future is in your hands. I just hope that you don't find that there are men that are growing up to be a man like you as we speak and they don't get their hands on her. She could be me fifteen years down the line or she could be Monica. Either way, she's in for it because you are her father."

"I understand why you would be bitter Pier. But you should know that I am filing for divorce. I want to start off fresh. Stacey and I want to put this nightmare behind us."

"Monica was alive when you got to the house. I was a bit out of it, but I remember telling you to call 911 and you didn't. I remember you taking her head and hitting it against the end table again. I can't prove it but I know what I saw."

"Things happen for a reason. That got on my last nerve with her nagging and always crying over my not wanting to be with her but you know what, that pussy, I just couldn't stay out of it. Was it worth not marrying and trying to have a family? No. But it was damn good when I didn't have anybody in my life. She pushed me. She went against things that I told her and tried to push my hand. She forgot that she had boundaries. I knew that the opportunity would present itself for me to get her out of my life once and for all. My thoughts were that she would get tired of me, meet somebody else and go live happily ever after. I would see my daughter when I could and the threat of her going to my job and causing trouble would be gone. But when I came home that night, something emotional came over me. All the frustration that I had been feeling wanted to come out. I needed to hit something. It was either her or you. You were hardly in as bad a shape as she was so she was the unlucky one that night."

"You're day will come Kyle." She got up to leave.

"Pier, hang in there. It won't be as bad as you think."

She kept her back to him as she was escorted out. Her head felt like it was about to burst. Her heart was beating so hard that she thought it too would explode. She went back to her cell where she stayed until the next morning when she met with her lawyer.

"Pier we can do this one of two ways. First, I want to tell you that I questioned Kyle again on his statement of what happened and he swears that Monica was dead when he got there."

"He's lying. He killed her."

"Pier I believe you. Do you want to go through a trial and possibly be convicted? I went to the prosecutor's office and they are willing to offer 3-5 years, a sentence term that is suitable for the crime given the surrounding circumstances."

"Three years?"

"Yes and with the possibility of parole after the third year. You can decline and go to trial but it would be against my advice. You and this woman had problems from the door. She lived with him as a nanny but that was lie. He told you that she was his daughter's mother and that made you angry. He allowed her to remain there and still have sex with her before and after you got married. You were jealous that he still wanted her, even with having you. All of this will point to you and paint you as a jealous wife who wanted his lover out of the picture. These are the things that will be said to you and about you. I'm here to help you. If you want to go to trial, we can do that but I think that this deal is as good as it's going to get and you should take it. We can move you to a different facility, one that is less restricted in that they have more and better activities and offer schooling as well. You will have a little more freedom. I'm afraid that if you elect to go to trial, the judge will not be as lenient and order you to stay here or worse, send you to Clinton."

"Okay, I'll take it." Pier said defeated.

"I'll contact the prosecutor's office, get the paperwork drawn up and signed and will be in touch. Pier,

with good behavior and a good attitude, you will get
through this time and before you know it, you will be
out. I'm sorry that you have to go through this. If you
ever need me or have any questions, you know how to
reach me."

Chapter Twenty-Three

Corrine, April and Renee made it their business to visit Pier twice a month at a facility that was located in southern Jersey. It was as her lawyer explained, nicer, cleaner and not a strict facility. The food was better and she was able to wear her own clothes. When they visited Pier, if she had a good week with no issues, she was able to sit outside and eat with them. They brought all of her favorite foods but had to take anything left over home with them. They also brought her clothes. Once they were searched, she could have them. Unfortunately, they weren't able to bring any pictures of Stacey because Kyle refused to communicate with Corrine. So the relationship that she had developed with Stacey became a sweet memory.

Pier took up scrap booking as a hobby since that was one of the two classes they offered. The other one, journaling, was her favorite. She would write and when they met weekly, she could express her feelings and what she felt when she wrote it. The class was designed to make inmates reflect on what they had done and to aid in the healing process. It proved to be therapeutic for her and she looked forward to the classes. While she wrote in her journal, she also sent Stacey letters. She wasn't sure if Kyle read them to her or not. However, they weren't returned to her either. She exercised daily and took an hour of her day to meditate. This kept her focused and help pass the time.

Linda became a frequent visitor to Pier too. For whatever reason, she felt bad that Pier had gotten mixed up with Kyle and ended up losing everything. They would talk about anything but Monica. Each of them had their own memory of the person that one called friend and the other thought an enemy so it wasn't spoken about. Linda would bring her magazines and prepackaged snacks. They were friends to each other in each other's time of need.

On holidays, Corrine, Renee, April and Linda would go to visit Pier together. They developed a bond with each other because they all had lost someone. They were able to have pictures taken and Pier would scrapbook them and show the others on their next visit. She managed to keep herself occupied to not think about how much time she had left. Surprisingly enough, at Christmas time, she got a card from Stacey. Receiving that card made Pier's heart smile. She continued to send her letters in the hopes that one day she would read them and remember their time together.

Kyle went through the dating process and when he found a woman that he thought he could control just like he did Monica and Pier, he moved her into his house. In the beginning she was just what he wanted, attentive, obedient and came to his every beck and call. He treated her like dirt and she didn't complain. He had no respect for her and after a few months into their relationship, he started cheating on her. When she found out, she confronted him and he admitted to being unfaithful. He tried to pull the "you knew how I was in the beginning" line on her, but she wasn't having it. She didn't say much of anything at that moment.

A few weeks went by and he had the nerve to bring a woman that he was sexing to the house thinking that his live-in girlfriend was off somewhere and wasn't due home for a while. When he came into the house and tried to go into his bedroom, he was shocked to find his girlfriend in the bed with another woman. He and the woman that he was with stood speechless. She busted out laughing and left.

Kyle tripped out. He dragged the woman that his girlfriend was in the bed with and threw her outside butt naked. He then went back into the house and forced himself on his girlfriend. She tried to fight him off, but he ended up raping her then he beat her up really bad. His ego couldn't allow for his woman to choose another woman over him.

When she was able to, his girlfriend went down to the station and filed charges on him. He was once again stripped of his weapons and put on desk duty. His trial was a speedy one and he was found guilty of rape and assault and had to do 18 months in the county jail. He lost his job, pension and his house. Stacey was initially going to be sent to a foster home because neither Kyle nor Monica had any known living relatives, but Kyle reached out to Corrine and she took her. That was good because then she was able to take her to see Pier and that allowed Stacey and Pier to pick up their relationship from where they left off.

When Kyle was released, he moved to a two bedroom apartment in Eatontown. To support himself and Stacey, he had to take a job as a mall security guard during the day and worked at Pathmark at night. Since Stacey had been with Corrine while he was away, he allowed her to stay there during the week to keep stability in her life and took her on the weekends.

Pier was released from her program early for good behavior after serving three years. She moved in with Corrine and Stacey and started putting her life back together. Since she had a record, she couldn't get a conventional job so she started a non-profit organization that helped wives of police officers who were mentally, emotionally or physically abused, get away from their husbands. She brought in Linda who handled the legal aspect of legal separation or divorce on a pro-bono basis.

Eventually her organization became recognized by local politicians who were running for office and had a vested interest to end domestic abuse specifically within the families of law enforcement officers. Together they formed an alliance and brought light to the abuse that police officers' wives were subjected to.

In most cases the wives of police officers made less money than their husbands, and some didn't work at all. That made them completely dependent. Their husbands played on that, dared them to leave and questioned with what money they were going to leave with. A huge purpose of Pier's organization, was to build up finances to aide women and children who were in abusive situations leave and get them set up in safe and affordable housing so that they could live a life void of abuse.